Greatest Short Stories

VOLUME IV

FOREIGN

P. F. COLLIER & SON CORPORATION

PUBLISHERS   NEW YORK

PRINTED IN THE UNITED STATES OF AMERICA

CONTENTS

PAGE

1. DELIVERANCE 5
   Max Nordau

2. THE OUTLAWS 21
   Selma Lagerlöf

3. THE DUEL 51
   Nikolai Dmitrievitch Teleshov

4. THE HANGING AT LA PIROCHE 61
   Alexandre Dumas, Fils

5. THE GRAY NUN 83
   Nataly von Eschstruth

6. THE FÊTE AT COQUEVILLE 107
   Émile Zola

7. A WORK OF ART 155
   Anton Pavlovitch Chekhov

8. THE BIT OF STRING 165
   Guy de Maupassant

9. A SCANDAL IN BOHEMIA 179
   A. Conan Doyle

10. LOVE AND BREAD 217
    Jean August Strindberg

11. THE SUICIDE CLUB 233
    Robert Louis Stevenson

CONTENTS

PAGE

12. THE FOUNTAIN OF YOUTH 281
   Rudolf Baumbach

13. BOLESS 297
   Maxim Gorki

14. THE SILVER CRUCIFIX 309
   Antonio Fogazzaro

15. THE MUMMY'S FOOT 325
   Théophile Gautier

16. THE END OF CANDIA 347
   Gabriele D'Annunzio

17. THE PRICE OF A LIFE 365
   Augustin Eugène Scribe

DELIVERANCE

BY MAX NORDAU

DELIVERANCE

BY MAX NORDAU

FOR an hour the first regiment of Dragoons of the Guard had been drawn up on level ground behind a screen of low bushes, waiting the order to engage. For some time the fighting appeared to have ceased around them. Only a shattered gun carriage and the ground, pierced with deep holes like newly dug graves, heaped about with soft, yellowish earth, gave the spot the look of a battlefield. But the conflict was evident enough to the ear. On all sides thundered the cannon, and from the right came also the rattling of musketry. The roar of battle rose and fell like the gamut of a great orchestra executing the "Storm Movement" of the Pastoral Symphony.

In the foreground, on a slight elevation, a group of officers were attentively examining the French position. One of them, a Major, stood a little apart smoking a cigarette and gazing dreamily into the distance. He might not, perhaps, have attracted a feminine observer, but a masculine eye would certainly have marked him as a man of striking intellect. He was about thirty, tall, slight, with cold gray eyes, a pale, thin face and pale, sarcastic lips, just shadowed by a delicate auburn mustache. This silent, self-contained man had about him an air of strange listlessness and disenchantment that made him in every way a contrast to the tanned, sunburnt young fellows who stood about him, all on fire with the eagerness of battle. Taking off his helmet, he passed his hand over his forehead. It was an aristocratic, well-kept hand, with slender, bloodless fingers. The whole appearance of this officer—which even a uniform could not disguise—was that of a person of exceptional distinction, and indeed he was a person of very great distinction, being no other than Prince Louis von Hockstein Falckenbourg Gerau, the head of what was once a family of reigning princes.

Early left an orphan, the Prince found himself when he came of age master of an almost unlimited fortune. From his mother, a musician of exquisite sensibility, he had inherited an artistic temperament and keen sense of the beautiful; while from his father, a haughty and somewhat eccentric noble, he had received a disposition of such violence and independence that it brooked no control from outside and recognized no law but its own will.

It will take no great effort of the imagination to see how the world had treated the young prince. The Court distinguished him with special attentions; the ladies petted him; the men sought him. In this hot-house atmosphere of high life he came quickly to maturity, and, like most children brought up among older persons without companions of their own age, he was of a thoughtful, even suspicious, temperament. As, in addition to this, he looked at everything from a critical, almost skeptical, point of view, insisting on getting to the bottom of every question, he did not make the mistake of most young men in his position—the mistake of thinking the attentions paid him homage to his own talent. Perfectly frank with himself, he recognized that they were paid to his title and fortune.

"What do these people really know of me?" he often asked himself, on coming home from some Court festival to the solitude of his magnificent palace.

"Nothing, and yet they scarcely wait for my mouth to open to applaud my speech! But if all the words I spoke this evening were written down and submitted to a man of sense, his honest verdict would have to be: 'Well, perhaps this fellow isn't exactly a fool, but he certainly is mighty little over mediocrity.' Yet the world persists in treating me as if I were somebody! But it is not *me*—Louis—that they are really concerned with, but only Prince von Hockstein," etc.

Louis was actually jealous of *the Prince*. The latter seemed to him an enemy, bent on thwarting and overshadowing his real self, and the noble ambition awoke in him to amount to something, in himself, apart from his rank and fortune.

7

But this was easier said than done; everywhere the Prince von Hockstein, etc., barred the way for Louis and would not let him pass. He enrolled himself at the University—the most aristocratic set among the students hastened to pay him court. The professors even, men whose genius until then he had revered, were overcome with joy when he appeared in their class-rooms, and addressed their words markedly to him. He soon had enough of this, and tried the army. His colonel thanked him for the honor he did the regiment in joining it; his superiors paid him flattering attentions; his fellow officers bored him. Then, too, the pettiness of garrison life was not much to his taste, so he quitted active service, but not until he had been rapidly promoted to the rank of major.

Of course, all this time women had played some part in his life. There were a few trifling affairs with actresses that did not go deep, and some passing flirtations with women of the world. These last he quickly found unbearable, for—except in being a thousand times more exacting— the great ladies amounted to no more than did the ballet girls.

One experience, however, came near being serious. The Prince, traveling incognito through the Black Forest to the watering-place of Norderney, chanced to take a place in the coupé of the diligence next to a lady also going to Norderney. She was of striking beauty and fascination, and the Prince was completely bewitched. He exerted himself immensely, but his attentions were all received with courteous indifference. Perhaps it was this indifference—a new experience—that charmed him. After he reached Norderney he continued to pay his court. He kept his incognito and simply called himself Herr von Gerau.

The lady was surrounded by a crowd of admirers, and accepted Louis's daily bouquets just as she did those of the others. She treated all her admirers with indifference, possibly to the Prince her manner was a shade colder than to the rest. At this critical moment, a certain great personage, an acquaintance of Louis, arrived at Norderney, and etiquette required the Prince to pay him a visit of ceremony in full dress uniform. Of course his name and rank could no longer be concealed. The fair lady beheld her admirer in his magnificent blue uniform, and learned who he really was. Immediately she had eyes for no one else, and seemed by smiles and glances to give him every encouragement and to ask pardon for her former neglect.

By way of answer, the Prince sent her a package containing his uniform and jeweled pin in the shape of a crown. These were accompanied by a note in which he declared he gave her in perpetuity and in sole proprietorship the only things she had cared for in him.

He was on the point of starting to hunt reindeer in Norway when the war of 1870 broke out. He immediately asked leave to join his regiment, and the request, of course, was at once granted. Patriotism and enthusiasm had very little to do with his action. He rejoined his regiment in the first place because it was the corect thing to do, and in the second because he hoped that war might possibly give him some new sensations. Was he again disappointed? He was inclined to think so. Now for two weeks he had been in the enemy's country, and he had had no extraordinary experience. When you have two good servants and unlimited money, even in a campaign there are few hardships, especially in a victorious army. As for heroic deeds, there had simply been no occasion for them. And the old weariness had come upon him again, as he stood in front of his regiment, smoking his cigarette.

The French artillery was now advancing upon the ditch, and their balls struck the German batteries that it defended, making great havoc. Two regiments of infantry were ordered to the support of the batteries.

Marching first came the Third Westphalians. They passed so near the group of officers that Prince Louis could distinguish each face, each expression. The poor fellows had been marching for fourteen hours under the burning August sun. They were covered with dust and sweat and their uniforms were soiled with mud. But in no way did these heroes betray their deadly

fatigue. Their eyes, reddened by the heat, flamed
with the enthusiasm of war, their dry throats
found strength to shout "Hurrah!" The whole
regiment forgot their fatigue, and seemed, as
they marched under fire, like men refreshed and
stimulated by a generous draft.

"Poor devils," thought the Prince, "they are
running to death as if it were a kermess dance.
What are they thinking about?—nothing, probably. They are driven on by a blind desire of
conquest. What good will victory do them?
How will it better their lot—if they have the luck
to escape death? Glory for Germany? Perhaps
for me that might be worth something, hardly
for them. Victory might add to the splendor of
my uniform. Still, I don't know, I wear it so
seldom. Perhaps if I go to Japan next year, the
Mikado will receive me better if I belong to a victorious nation, but whether we beat the French
or they beat us, I suspect I will always get the
same welcome at the Jockey Club in Paris and
the Mediterranean Club in Nice. But those no-
bodies over there, what will their glorious and
victorious country do for them? They won't get
much of it in their village. All they know of the
'Fatherland' is the taxgatherers and the police,
and they will be what they have always been.
And yet there they are full of enthusiasm, I can't
deny it—it shakes even me. Well, we ought to
thank the poets who sing about patriotism and
military glory, and the schoolmasters who teach

the people's hearts the poets' words. Marvelous power of a word that can lead a prosaic peasant to give his life for an abstraction, an imagination!"

But even as with the quickness of lightning these thoughts passed through his mind, the Prince felt a sensation that amazed him. It was a feeling of confusion, of shame. It seemed as if he had been speaking his thoughts aloud and as if a group of grave and noble figures had listened to his words, and were now looking at him in a silence full of pity and disdain. Down in the depths of his soul, where the mocking light of his skeptical spirit failed to penetrate, he seemed to hear an imperial voice rebuking him and silencing his doubt.

"I am right," his mind said.

"You are wrong," declared the voice.

"Well, anyway, I shall not deceive *myself* with romantic dreams," cried Reason; but already it seemed to the Prince that the words were spoken by a stranger, and he shrank back from them indignantly.

By this time the Third Westphalians had covered the entire slope of the ditch, the sharpshooters were already at the top. There was a moment's hesitation, for the first heads that appeared above the ditch called forth a deadly fire from the enemy. Several men fell, but those behind pressed on, and in spite of their terrible fatigue, tried with hands and feet to make the ascent that would have been play to men in good condition. As they marched on, all on fire with noble ardor, Heine's words came back to the Prince: "How I love the dear, good Westphalians! They are so sure, so firm, so faithful. It is magnificent to see them on the field of battle, those heroes, with their lion hearts."

Pushed on by their "lion hearts," the Westphalians continued to scramble up the slope, expending their last breath in the effort to go forward. But the French, maddened by this outburst, forced them, after a terrible combat man to man, to recoil to the bottom of the ditch, which began to fill up with heaps of dead and wounded. The survivors tried to retreat up the other slope, and now the spectators above beheld a heartrending sight. The men were so completely exhausted that they could not make the easy ascent. The muskets fell from their hands, and the French made many prisoners.

Above there was the greatest excitement. The Eighth Westphalians arrived, commanded by the General in person, and started immediately to the aid of its comrades. The French were forced back and many prisoners were recaptured. But the advantage was of short duration. New masses of the enemy's infantry were coming up, and in the distance the cavalry were seen approaching.

Prince Louis had followed the combat with increasing emotion—he felt his heart beat alter-

nately with joy and fear. It seemed to him now
that the critical moment had come, and he read
the same impression in the faces of the other
officers. The Colonel called his orderly and
sprang into the saddle. The trumpets sounded,
and a sudden movement passed through the
regiment. In a moment every one was on horse-
back, sabres clinked against the spurs, the horses
neighed. Again the trumpets sounded and the
whole troop began the march.

Prince Louis glanced at his watch—it was half-
past six in the evening. As he rode along at the
head of the first squadron, a short distance from
the Colonel and adjutants, he felt himself seized
by a sensation he had never in his life experienced. The madness, the feverish impatience of a
moment before had melted away with the consciousness of acting for a given purpose. The
knowledge of activity, of seeking a definite end,
brought him rest. He stopped looking for reasons; he thought no more of criticizing. The
spirit of doubt was driven out of him. He
obeyed with the ardor, the belief, the simple
obedience of a child, the irresistible command
that was pushing his entire being forward. This
man, so proud of his *ego,* he, who had always
sought happiness by the unlimited activity of his
personal will, now found that will so crushed and
bound that it was scarcely perceptible. A Power,
call it Natural Law, call it the Divine Will, that
is ever manifesting itself by the course of history,

had entered into him and taken possession of him. He was no longer master of his destiny, he was taken out of himself by a stranger—was it a supernatural vision, a great genius, a Delivering Christ?—Louis felt himself only a screw, a rivet in the machinery of the world's history, and strange to say this dissolving of his individuality in a great whole, as complete as the melting of a piece of sugar in a glass of water, caused him neither sorrow nor regret. On the contrary, a strange pleasure penetrated his entire being and made him tremble with joy. He felt himself very small, yet at the same time he saw in himself something great that transcended the limit of his own personality. In a word, he had found at last that sensation he had always desired. He was delivered from his prison of egotism and at large among great generalities.

The regiment was now descending the slope, avoiding the heaps of dead and wounded. The horses quickly ascended the opposite side and, the trumpets sounding, the regiment separated into two lines and advanced.

What followed might have been taken for a representation of the conflict of the gods in Valhalla. The French cuirassiers, riding toward the sun, were illumined with an unearthly light, their shining sabres seemed like tongues of flame, their cuirasses and helmets shone like white-hot steel. The German dragoons had their backs to the sun, and the long black shadows of horses and horse-

THE OUTLAWS

BY SELMA LAGERLÖF

THE OUTLAWS

BY SELMA LAGERLÖF

A PEASANT had killed a monk and fled to the woods. He became an outlaw, upon whose head a price was set. In the forest he met another fugitive, a young fisherman from one of the outermost islands, who had been accused of the theft of a herring net. The two became companions, cut themselves a home in a cave, laid their nets together, cooked their food, made their arrows, and held watch one for the other. The peasant could never leave the forest. But the fisherman, whose crime was less serious, would now and then take upon his back the game they had killed, and would creep down to the more isolated houses on the outskirts of the village. In return for milk, butter, arrow-heads, and clothing he would sell his game, the black mountain cock, the moor hen, with her shining feathers, the toothsome doe, and the long-eared hare.

The cave which was their home cut down deep into a mountain-side. The entrance was guarded by wide slabs of stone and ragged thorn-bushes. High up on the hillside there stood a giant pine,

Translated by Grace Isabel Colbron. Copyright, 1907, by P. F. Collier & Son.

and the chimney of the fireplace nestled among its coiled roots. Thus the smoke could draw up through the heavy hanging branches and fade unseen into the air. To reach their cave the men had to wade through the stream that sprang out from the hill slope. No pursuer thought of seeking their trail in this merry brooklet. At first they were hunted as wild animals are. The peasants of the district gathered to pursue them as if for a baiting of wolf or bear. The bowmen surrounded the wood while the spear carriers entered and left no thicket or ravine unsearched. The two outlaws cowered in their gloomy cave, panting in terror and listening breathlessly as the hunt passed on with noise and shouting over the mountain ranges.

For one long day the young fisherman lay motionless, but the murderer could stand it no longer, and went out into the open where he could see his enemy. They discovered him and set after him, but this was far more to his liking than lying quiet in impotent terror. He fled before his pursuers, leaped the streams, slid down the precipices, climbed up perpendicular walls of rock. All his remarkable strength and skill awoke to energy under the spur of danger. His body became as elastic as a steel spring, his foot held firm, his hand grasped sure, his eye and ear were doubly sharp. He knew the meaning of every murmur in the foliage; he could understand the warning in an upturned stone.

When he had clambered up the side of a preci-
pice he would stop to look down on his pursuers,
greeting them with loud songs of scorn. When
their spears sang above him in the air, he would
catch them and hurl them back. As he crashed
his way through tangled underbrush something
within him seemed to sing a wild song of rejoicing. A gaunt, bare hilltop stretched itself
through the forest, and all alone upon its crest
there stood a towering pine. The red brown
trunk was bare, in the thick grown boughs at the
top a hawk's nest rocked in the breeze. So daring had the fugitive grown that on another day
he climbed to the nest while his pursuers sought
him in the woody slopes below. He sat there and
twisted the necks of the young hawks as the hunt
raged far beneath him. The old birds flew scream-
ing about him in anger. They swooped past his
face, they struck at his eyes with their beaks, beat
at him with their powerful wings, and clawed
great scratches in his weather-hardened skin.
He battled with them laughing. He stood up
in the rocking nest as he lunged at the birds with
his knife, and he lost all thought of danger and
pursuit in the joy of the battle. When recollec-
tion came again and he turned to look for his
enemies, the hunt had gone off in another direction. Not one of the pursuers had thought of
raising his eyes to the clouds to see the prey
hanging there, doing schoolboy deeds of reckless-
ness while his life hung in the balance. But the

man trembled from head to foot when he saw that he was safe. He caught for a support with his shaking hands; he looked down giddily from the height to which he had climbed. Groaning in fear of a fall, afraid of the birds, afraid of the possibility of being seen, weakened through terror of everything and anything, he slid back down the tree trunk. He laid himself flat upon the earth and crawled over the loose stones until he reached the underbrush. There he hid among the tangled branches of the young pines, sinking down, weak and helpless, upon the soft moss. A single man might have captured him.

. . . .

Tord was the name of the fisherman. He was but sixteen years old, but was strong and brave. He had now lived for a whole year in the wood.

The peasant's name was Berg, and they had called him "The Giant." He was handsome and well-built, the tallest and strongest man in the entire county. He was broad-shouldered and yet slender. His hands were delicate in shape, as if they had never known hard work, his hair was brown, his face soft-colored. When he had lived for some time in the forest his look of strength was awe-inspiring. His eyes grew piercing under bushy brows wrinkled by great muscles over the forehead. His lips were more firmly set than before, his face more haggard, with deepened hollows at the temples, and his strongly marked cheek-bones stood out plainly. All the softer curves of his body disappeared, but the muscles grew strong as steel. His hair turned gray rapidly.

Tord had never seen any one so magnificent and so mighty before. In his imagination, his companion towered high as the forest, strong as the raging surf. He served him humbly, as he would have served a master, he revered him as he would have revered a god. It seemed quite natural that Tord should carry the hunting spear, that he should drag the game home, draw the water, and build the fire. Berg, the Giant, accepted all these services, but scarce threw the boy a friendly word. He looked upon him with contempt, as a common thief.

The outlaws did not live by pillage, but supported themselves by hunting and fishing. Had not Berg killed a holy man, the peasants would soon have tired of the pursuit and left them to themselves in the mountains. But they feared disaster for the villages if he who had laid hands upon a servant of God should go unpunished. When Tord took his game down into the valley they would offer him money and a pardon for himself if he would lead them to the cave of the Giant, that they might catch the latter in his sleep. But the boy refused, and if they followed him he would lead them astray until they gave up the pursuit.

Once Berg asked him whether the peasants had ever tried to persuade him to betrayal. When he learned what reward they had promised he said scornfully that Tord was a fool not to accept such offers. Tord looked at him with something in his eyes that Berg, the Giant, had never seen before. No beautiful woman whom he had loved in the days of his youth had ever looked at him like that; not even in the eyes of his own children, or of his wife, had he seen such affection. "You are my God, the ruler I have chosen of my own free will." This was what the eyes said. "You may scorn me, or beat me, if you will, but I shall still remain faithful."

From this on Berg gave more heed to the boy and saw that he was brave in action but shy in speech. Death seemed to have no terrors for him. He would deliberately choose for his path the fresh formed ice on the mountain pools, the treacherous surface of the morass in springtime. He seemed to delight in danger. It gave him some compensation for the wild ocean storms he could no longer go out to meet. He would tremble in the night darkness of the wood, however, and even by day the gloom of a thicket or a deeper shadow could frighten him. When Berg asked him about this he was silent in embarrassment.

Tord did not sleep in the bed by the hearth at the back of the cave, but every night, when Berg was asleep the boy would creep to the entrance and lie there on one of the broad stones. Berg discovered this, and although he guessed the reason he asked the boy about it. Tord would not answer. To avoid further questions he slept in the bed for two nights, then returned to his post at the door.

One night, when a snow-storm raged in the tree-tops, piling up drifts even in the heart of the thickets, the flakes swirled into the cave of the outlaws. Tord, lying by the entrance, awoke in the morning to find himself wrapped in a blanket of melting snow. A day or two later he fell ill. Sharp pains pierced his lungs when he tried to draw breath. He endured the pain as long as his strength would stand it, but one evening, when he stooped to blow up the fire, he fell down and could not rise again. Berg came to his side and told him to lie in the warm bed. Tord groaned in agony, but could not move. Berg put his arm under the boy's body and carried him to the bed. He had a feeling while doing it as if he were touching a clammy snake; he had a taste in his mouth as if he had eaten unclean horseflesh, so repulsive was it to him to touch the person of this common thief. Berg covered the sick boy with his own warm bear-skin rug and gave him water. This was all he could do, but the illness was not dangerous, and Tord recovered quickly. But now that Berg had had to do his companion's work for a few days, and had had to care for him, they seemed to have come nearer to one another. Tord dared to speak to Berg sometimes, as they sat together by the fire cutting their arrows.

"You come of good people, Berg," Tord said one evening. "Your relatives are the richest peasants in the valley. The men of your name have served kings and fought in their castles."

"They have more often fought with the rebels and done damage to the king's property," answered Berg.

"Your forefathers held great banquets at Christmas time. And you held banquets too, when you were at home in your house. Hundreds of men and women could find place on the benches in your great hall, the hall that was built in the days before St. Olaf came here to Viken for christening. Great silver urns were there, and mighty horns, filled with mead, went the rounds of your table."

Berg looked at the boy again. He sat on the edge of the bed with his head in his hands, pushing back the heavy tangled hair that hung over his eyes. His face had become pale and refined through his illness. His eyes still sparkled in fever. He smiled to himself at the pictures called up by his fancy—pictures of the great hall and of the silver urns, of the richly clad guests, and of Berg, the Giant, lording it in the place of honor. The peasant knew that even in the days of his glory no one had ever looked at him with eyes so shining in admiration, so glowing in reverence, as this boy did now, as he sat by the fire in his worn leather jacket. He was touched, and

yet displeased. This common thief had no right
to admire him.

"Were there no banquets in your home?" he
asked.

Tord laughed: "Out there on the rocks where
father and mother live? Father plunders the
wrecks and mother is a witch. When the weather
is stormy she rides out to meet the ships on a
seal's back, and those who are washed overboard
from the wrecks belong to her."

"What does she do with them?" asked Berg.

"Oh, a witch always needs corpses. She makes
salves of them, or perhaps she eats them. On
moonlit nights she sits out in the wildest surf and
looks for the eyes and fingers of drowned
children."

"That is horrible!" said Berg.

The boy answered with calm confidence: "It
would be for others, but not for a witch. She
can't help it."

This was an altogether new manner of looking
at life for Berg. "Then thieves have to steal, as
witches have to make magic?" he questioned
sharply.

"Why, yes," answered the boy. "Every one
has to do the thing he was born for." But a smile
of shy cunning curled his lips, as he added:
"There are thieves who have never stolen."

"What do you mean by that?" spoke Berg.

The boy still smiled his mysterious smile and
seemed happy to have given his companion a

riddle. "There are birds that do not fly; and there are thieves who have not stolen," he said.

Berg feigned stupidity, in order to trick the other's meaning: "How can any one be called a thief who has never stolen?" he said.

The boy's lips closed tight as if to hold back the words. "But if one has a father who steals—" he threw out after a short pause.

"A man may inherit house and money, but the name thief is given only to him who earns it."

Tord laughed gently. "But when one has a mother—and that mother comes and cries, and begs one to take upon one's self the father's crime—and then one can laugh at the hangman and run away into the woods. A man may be outlawed for the sake of a fish net he has never seen."

Berg beat his fist upon the stone table, in great anger. Here this strong, beautiful boy had thrown away his whole life for another. Neither love, nor riches, nor the respect of his fellow men could ever be his again. The sordid care for food and clothing was all that remained to him in life. And this fool had let him, Berg, despise an innocent man. He scolded sternly, but Tord was not frightened any more than a sick child is frightened at the scolding of his anxious mother.

. . . .

High up on one of the broad wooded hills there lay a black swampy lake. It was square in shape,

and its banks were as straight, and their corners
as sharp as if it had been the work of human
hands. On three sides steep walls of rock rose up,
with hardy mountain pines clinging to the stones,
their roots as thick as a man's arm. At the surface of the lake, where the few strips of grass
had been washed away, these naked roots twisted
and coiled, rising out of the water like myriad
snakes that had tried to escape from the waves,
but had been turned to stone in their struggle.
Or was it more like a mass of blackened skeletons
of long-drowned giants which the lake was trying to throw off? The arms and legs were twisted
in wild contortions, the long fingers grasped deep
into the rocks, the mighty ribs formed arches
that upheld ancient trees. But now and again
these iron-hard arms, these steel fingers with
which the climbing pines supported themselves,
would loosen their hold, and then the strong
north wind would hurl the tree from the ridge
far out into the swamp. There it would lie, its
crown burrowing deep in the muddy water. The
fishes found good hiding places amid its twigs,
while the roots rose up over the water like the
arms of some hideous monster, giving the little
lake a repulsive appearance.

The mountains sloped down on the fourth side
of the little lake. A tiny rivulet foamed out here;
but before the stream could find its path it twisted
and turned among boulders and mounds of earth,
forming a whole colony of islands, some of which

scarce offered foothold, while others carried as many as twenty trees on their back.

Here, where the rocks were not high enough to shut out the sun, the lighter foliaged trees could grow. Here were the timid, gray-green alders, and the willows with their smooth leaves. Birches were here, as they always are wherever there is a chance to shut out the evergreens, and there were mountain ash and elder bushes, giving charm and fragrance to the place.

At the entrance to the lake there was a forest of rushes as high as a man's head, through which the sunlight fell as green upon the water as it falls on the moss in the true forest. There were little clearings among the reeds, little round ponds where the water lilies slumbered. The tall rushes looked down with gentle gravity upon these sensitive beauties, who closed their white leaves and their yellow hearts so quickly in their leather outer dress as soon as the sun withdrew his rays.

One sunny day the outlaws came to one of these little ponds to fish. They waded through the reeds to two high stones, and sat there throwing out their bait for the big green, gleaming pike that slumbered just below the surface of the water. These men, whose life was now passed entirely among the mountains and the woods, had come to be as completely under the control of the powers of nature as were the plants or the animals. When the sun shone they were open-hearted and merry, at evening they became silent, and the night, which seemed to them so all-powerful, robbed them of their strength. And now the green light that fell through the reeds and drew out from the water stripes of gold, brown, and black-green, smoothed them into a sort of magic mood. They were completely shut out from the outer world. The reeds swayed gently in the soft wind, the rushes murmured, and the long, ribbon-like leaves struck them lightly in the face. They sat on the gray stones in their gray leather garments, and the shaded tones of the leather melted into the shades of the stones. Each saw his comrade sitting opposite him as quietly as a stone statue. And among the reeds they saw giant fish swimming, gleaming and glittering in all colors of the rainbow. When the men threw out their lines and watched the rings on the water widen amid the reeds, it seemed to them that the motion grew and grew until they saw it was not they themselves alone that had occasioned it. A Nixie, half human, half fish, lay sleeping deep down in the water. She lay on her back, and the waves clung so closely to her body that the men had not seen her before. It was her breath that stirred the surface. But it did not seem to the watchers that there was anything strange in the fact that she lay there. And when she had disappeared in the next moment they did not know whether her appearance had been an illusion or not.

The green light pierced through their eyes into their brains like a mild intoxication. They saw visions among the reeds, visions which they would not tell even to each other. There was not much fishing done. The day was given up to dreams and visions.

A sound of oars came from among the reeds, and they started up out of their dreaming. In a few moments a heavy boat, hewn out of a tree trunk, came into sight, set in motion by oars not much broader than walking sticks. The oars were in the hands of a young girl who had been gathering water-lilies. She had long, dark brown braids of hair, and great dark eyes, but she was strangely pale, a pallor that was not gray, but softly pink tinted. Her cheeks were no deeper in color than the rest of her face; her lips were scarce redder. She wore a bodice of white linen and a leather belt with a golden clasp. Her skirt was of blue with a broad red hem. She rowed past close by the outlaws without seeing them. They sat absolutely quiet, less from fear of discovery than from the desire to look at her undisturbed. When she had gone, the stone statues became men again and smiled:

"She was as white as the water-lilies," said one. "And her eyes were as dark as the water back there under the roots of the pines."

They were both so merry that they felt like laughing, like really laughing as they had never laughed in this swamp before, a laugh that would echo back from the wall of rock and loosen the roots of the pines.

"Did you think her beautiful?" asked the Giant.

"I do not know, she passed so quickly. Perhaps she was beautiful."

"You probably did not dare to look at her. Did you think she was the Nixie?"

And again they felt a strange desire to laugh.

. . . .

While a child, Tord had once seen a drowned man. He had found the corpse on the beach in broad daylight, and it had not frightened him, but at night his dreams were terrifying. He had seemed to be looking out over an ocean, every wave of which threw a dead body at his feet. He saw all the rocks and islands covered with corpses of the drowned, the drowned that were dead and belonged to the sea, but that could move, and speak, and threaten him with their white stiffened fingers.

And so it was again. The girl whom he had seen in the reeds appeared to him in his dreams. He met her again down at the bottom of the swamp lake, where the light was greener even than in the reeds, and there he had time enough to see that she was beautiful. He dreamed that he sat on one of the great pine roots in the midst of the lake while the tree rocked up and down, now under, now over the surface of the water. Then he saw her on one of the smallest islands.

She stood under the red mountain ash and laughed at him. In his very last dream it had gone so far that she had kissed him. But then it was morning, and he heard Berg rising, but he kept his eyes stubbornly closed that he might continue to dream. When he did awake he was dazed and giddy from what he had seen during the night. He thought much more about the girl than he had done the day before. Toward evening it occurred to him to ask Berg if he knew her name.

Berg looked at him sharply. "It is better for you to know it at once," he said. "It was Unn. We are related to each other."

And then Tord knew that it was this pale maiden who was the cause of Berg's wild hunted life in forest and mountain. He tried to search his memory for what he had heard about her.

Unn was the daughter of a free peasant. Her mother was dead, and she ruled in her father's household. This was to her taste, for she was independent by nature, and had no inclination to give herself to any husband. Unn and Berg were cousins, and the rumor had long gone about that Berg liked better to sit with Unn and her maids than to work at home in his own house. One Christmas, when the great banquet was to be given in Berg's hall, his wife had invited a monk from Draksmark, who, she hoped, would show Berg how wrong it was that he should neglect her for another. Berg and others besides him hated this monk because of his appearance. He was very stout and absolutely white. The ring of hair around his bald head, the brows above his moist eyes, the color of his skin, of his hands, and of his garments, were all white. Many found him very repulsive to look at.

But the monk was fearless, and as he believed that his words would have greater weight if many heard them, he rose at the table before all the guests, and said: "Men call the cuckoo the vilest of birds because he brings up his young in the nest of others. But here sits a man who takes no care for his house and his children, and who seeks his pleasure with a strange woman. Him I will call the vilest of men." Unn rose in her place. "Berg, this is said to you and to me," she cried. "Never have I been so shamed, but my father is not here to protect me." She turned to go, but Berg hurried after her. "Stay where you are," she said. "I do not wish to see you again." He stopped her in the corridor, and asked her what he should do that she might stay with him. Her eyes glowed as she answered that he himself should know best what he must do. Then Berg went into the hall again and slew the monk.

Berg and Tord thought on awhile with the same thoughts, then Berg said: "You should have seen her when the white monk fell. My wife drew the children about her and cursed Unn. She turned the faces of the children toward her, that they might always remember the woman for whose sake their father had become a murderer. But Unn stood there so quiet and so beautiful that the men who saw her trembled. She thanked me for the deed, and prayed me to flee to the woods at once. She told me never to become a robber, and to use my knife only in some cause equally just."

"Your deed had ennobled her," said Tord.

And again Berg found himself astonished at the same thing that had before now surprised him in the boy. Tord was a heathen, or worse than a heathen; he never condemned that which was wrong. He seemed to know no sense of responsibility. What had to come, came. He knew of God, of Christ, and the Saints, but he knew them only by name, as one knows the names of the gods of other nations. The ghosts of the Scheeren Islands were his gods. His mother, learned in magic, had taught him to believe in the spirits of the dead. And then it was that Berg undertook a task which was as foolish as if he had woven a rope for his own neck. He opened the eyes of this ignorant boy to the power of God, the Lord of all Justice, the avenger of wrong who condemned sinners to the pangs of hell everlasting. And he taught him to love Christ and His Mother, and all the saintly men and women who sit before the throne of God praying that His anger may be turned away from sinners. He taught him all that mankind has learned to do to soften the wrath of God. He told him of the long trains of pilgrims journeying to the holy places; he told him of those who scourged themselves in their remorse; and he told him of the pious monks who flee the joys of this world.

The longer he spoke the paler grew the boy and the keener his attention as his eyes widened at the visions. Berg would have stopped, but the torrent of his own thoughts carried him away. Night sank down upon them, the black forest night, where the scream of the owl shrills ghostly through the stillness. God came so near to them that the brightness of His throne dimmed the stars, and the angels of vengeance descended upon the mountain heights. And below them the flames of the underworld fluttered up to the outer curve of the earth and licked greedily at this last refuge of a race crushed by sin and woe.

.   .   .   .

Autumn came, and with it came storm. Tord went out alone into the woods to tend the traps and snares, while Berg remained at home to mend his clothes. The boy's path led him up a wooded height along which the falling leaves danced in circles in the gust. Again and again the feeling came to him that some one was walking behind him. He turned several times, then went on again when he had seen that it was only the wind and the leaves. He threatened the rustling circles with his fist, and kept on his way. But he had not silenced the sounds of his vision. At first it was the little dancing feet of elfin children; then it was the hissing of a great snake moving up behind him. Beside the snake there came a wolf, a tall, gray creature, waiting for the moment when the adder should strike at his feet to spring upon his back. Tord hastened his steps, but the visions hastened with him. When they seemed but two steps behind him, ready for the spring, he turned. There was nothing there, as he had known all the time. He sat down upon a stone to rest. The dried leaves played about his feet. The leaves of all the forest trees were there: the little yellow birch leaves, the red-tinged mountain ash leaves, the dried, black-brown foliage of the elm, the bright red aspen leaves, and the yellow-green fringes of the willows. Faded and crumpled, broken, and scarred, they were but little like the soft, tender shoots of green that had unrolled from the buds a few months ago.

"Ye are sinners," said the boy. "All of us are sinners. Nothing is pure in the eyes of God. Ye have already been shriveled up in the flame of His wrath."

Then he went on again, while the forest beneath him waved like a sea in storm, although it was still and calm on the path around him. But he heard something he had never heard before. The wood was full of voices. Now it was like a whispering, now a gentle plaint, now a loud threat, or a roaring curse. It laughed, and it moaned. It was as the voice of hundreds. This unknown something that threatened and excited, that whistled and hissed, a something that seemed to be, and yet was not, almost drove him mad. He shivered in deadly terror, as he had shivered before, the day that he lay on the floor of his cave, and heard his pursuers rage over him through the forest. He seemed to hear again the crashing of the branches, the heavy footsteps of the men, the clanking of their arms, and their wild, bloodthirsty shouts.

It was not alone the storm that roared about him. There was something else in it, something yet more terrible; there were voices he could not understand, sounds as of a strange speech. He had heard many a mightier storm than this roar through the rigging. But he had never heard the wind playing on a harp of so many strings. Every tree seemed to have its own voice, every ravine had another song, the loud echo from the rocky wall shouted back in its own voice. He knew all these tones, but there were other stranger noises with them. And it was these that awoke a storm of voices within his own brain.

He had always been afraid when alone in the darkness of the wood. He loved the open sea and the naked cliffs. Ghosts and spirits lurked here in the shadows of the trees.

Then suddenly he knew who was speaking to him in the storm. It was God, the Great Avenger, the Lord of all Justice. God pursued him because of his comrade. God demanded that he should give up the murderer of the monk to vengeance.

Tord began to speak aloud amid the storm. He told God what he wanted to do, but that he could not do it. He had wanted to speak to the Giant and to beg him make his peace with God. But he could not find the words; embarrassment tied his tongue. "When I learned that the world is ruled by a God of Justice," he cried, "I knew that he was a lost man. I have wept through the night for my friend. I know that God will find him no matter where he may hide. But I could not speak to him; I could not find the words because of my love for him. Do not ask that I shall speak to him. Do not ask that the ocean shall rise to the height of the mountains."

He was silent again, and the deep voice of the storm, which he knew for God's voice, was silent also. There was a sudden pause in the wind, a burst of sunshine, a sound as of oars, and the gentle rustling of stiff reeds. These soft tones brought up the memory of Unn.

Then the storm began again, and he heard steps behind him, and a breathless panting. He did not dare to turn this time, for he knew that it was the white monk. He came from the banquet in Berg's great hall, covered with blood, and with an open ax cut in his forehead. And he whispered: "Betray him. Give him up, that you may save his soul."

Tord began to run. All this terror grew and

grew in him, and he tried to flee from it. But as he ran he heard behind him the deep, mighty voice, which he knew was the voice of God. It was God himself pursuing him, demanding that he should give up the murderer. Berg's crime seemed more horrible to him than ever it had seemed before. A weaponless man had been murdered, a servant of God cut down by the steel. And the murderer still dared to live. He dared to enjoy the light of the sun and the fruits of the earth. Tord halted, clinched his fists, and shrieked a threat. Then, like a madman, he ran from the forest, the realm of terror, down into the valley.

. . . .

When Tord entered the cave the outlaw sat upon the bench of stone, sewing. The fire gave but a pale light, and the work did not seem to progress satisfactorily. The boy's heart swelled in pity. This superb Giant seemed all at once so poor and so unhappy.

"What is the matter?" asked Berg. "Are you ill? Have you been afraid?"

Then for the first time Tord spoke of his fear. "It was so strange in the forest. I heard the voices of spirits and I saw ghosts. I saw white monks."

"Boy!"

"They sang to me all the way up the slope to the hilltop. I ran from them, but they ran after me, singing. Can I not lay the spirits? What have I to do with them? There are others to whom their appearance is more necessary."

"Are you crazy to-night, Tord?"

Tord spoke without knowing what words he was using. His shyness had left him all at once, speech seemed to flow from his lips. "They were white monks, as pale as corpses. And their clothes are spotted with blood. They draw their hoods down over their foreheads, but I can see the wound shining there. The great, yawning, red wound from the ax."

"Tord," said the giant, pale and deeply grave, "the Saints alone know why you see wounds of ax thrusts. I slew the monk with a knife."

Tord stood before Berg trembling and wringing his hands. "They demand you of me. They would compel me to betray you."

"Who? The monks?"

"Yes, yes, the monks. They show me visions. They show me Unn. They show me the open, sunny ocean. They show me the camps of the fishermen, where there is dancing and merriment. I close my eyes, and yet I can see it all. 'Leave me,' I say to them. 'My friend has committed a murder, but he is not bad. Leave me alone, and I will talk to him, that he may repent and atone. He will see the wrong he has done, and he will make a pilgrimage to the Holy Grave.'"

"And what do the monks answer?" asked Berg. "They do not want to pardon me. They want to torture me and to burn me at the stake."

44

" 'Shall I betray my best friend?' I ask them.
He is all that I have in the world. He saved me
from the bear when its claws were already at my
throat. We have suffered hunger and cold together. He covered me with his own garments
while I was ill. I have brought him wood and
water, I have watched over his sleep and led his
enemies off the trail. Why should they think
me a man who betrays his friend? My friend
will go to the priest himself, and will confess to
him, and then together we will seek absolution."

Berg listened gravely, his keen eyes searching
in Tord's face. "Go to the priest yourself, and
tell him the truth. You must go back again
among mankind."

"What does it help if I go alone? The spirits
of the dead follow me because of your sin. Do
you not see how I tremble before you? You have
lifted your hand against God himself. What
crime is like unto yours? Why did you tell me
about the just God? It is you yourself who compel me to betray you. Spare me this sin. Go to
the priest yourself." He sank down on his knees
before Berg.

The murderer laid his hand on his head and
looked at him. He measured his sin by the terror
of his comrade, and it grew and grew to monstrous size. He saw himself in conflict with the
Will that rules the world. Remorse entered his
heart.

"Woe unto me that I did what I did," he said.

"And is not this miserable life, this life we lead here in terror, and in deprivation, is it not atonement enough? Have I not lost home and fortune? Have I not lost friends, and all the joys that make the life of a man? What more?"

As he heard him speak thus, Tord sprang up in wild terror. "You can repent!" he cried. "My words move your heart? Oh, come with me, come at once. Come, let us go while yet there is time."

Berg the Giant sprang up also. "You—did it—?"

"Yes, yes, yes. I have betrayed you. But come quickly. Come now, now that you can repent. We must escape. We will escape."

The murderer stooped to the ground where the battle-ax of his fathers lay at his feet. "Son of a thief," he hissed. "I trusted you—I loved you."

But when Tord saw him stoop for the ax, he knew that it was his own life that was in peril now. He tore his own ax from his girdle, and thrust at Berg before the latter could rise. The Giant fell headlong to the floor, the blood spurting out over the cave. Between the tangled masses of hair Tord saw the great, yawning, red wound of an ax thrust.

Then the peasants stormed into the cave. They praised his deed and told him that he should receive full pardon.

Tord looked down at his hands, as if he saw there the fetters that had drawn him on to kill the man he loved. Like the chains of the Fenrir wolf, they were woven out of empty air. They were woven out of the green light amid the reeds, out of the play of shadows in the woods, out of the song of the storm, out of the rustling of the leaves, out of the magic vision of dreams. And he said aloud: "God is great."

He crouched beside the body, spoke amid his tears to the dead, and begged him to awake. The villagers made a litter of their spears, on which to carry the body of the free peasant to his home. The dead man aroused awe in their souls, they softened their voices in his presence. When they raised him on to the bier, Tord stood up, shook the hair from his eyes, and spoke in a voice that trembled:

"Tell Unn, for whose sake Berg the Giant became a murderer, that Tord the fisherman, whose father plunders wrecks, and whose mother is a witch—tell her that Tord slew Berg because Berg had taught him that justice is the cornerstone of the world."

THE DUEL

BY NIKOLAI DMITRIEVITCH TELESHOV

THE DUEL

BY NIKOLAI DMITRIEVITCH TELESHOV

I T WAS early morning—
Vladimir Kladunov, a tall, graceful young
man, twenty-two years of age, almost boy-
ish in appearance, with a handsome face and
thick, fair curls, dressed in the uniform of an
officer and in long riding boots, minus overcoat
and cap, stood upon a meadow covered with new-
fallen snow, and gazed at another officer, a tall,
red-faced, mustached man, who faced him at a
distance of thirty paces, and was slowly lifting
his hand in which he held a revolver, and aimed
it straight at Vladimir.

With his arms crossed over his breast and also
holding in one hand a revolver, Kladunov, almost
with indifference, awaited the shot of his oppon-
ent. His handsome, young face, though a little
paler than usual, was alight with courage, and
wore a scornful smile. His dangerous position,
and the merciless determination of his adversary,
the strenuous attention of the seconds who silently stood at one side, and the imminence of
death, made the moment one of terrible intensity
—mysterious, almost solemn. A question of
honor was to be decided. Every one felt the im-

Translated by Lizzie B. Gorin. Copyright, 1907, by P. F. Collier & Son.

portance of the question; the less they understood what they were doing, the deeper seemed the solemnity of the moment.

A shot was fired; a shiver ran through all. Vladimir threw his hands about, bent his knees, and fell. He lay upon the snow, shot through the head, his hands apart, his hair, face, and even the snow around his head covered with blood. The seconds ran toward him and lifted him; the doctor certified his death, and the question of honor was solved. It only remained to announce the news to the regiment and to inform, as tenderly and carefully as possible, the mother, who was now left alone in the world, for the boy that had been killed was her only son. Before the duel no one had given her even a thought; but now they all became very thoughtful. All knew and loved her, and recognized the fact that she must be prepared by degrees for the terrible news. At last Ivan Golubenko was chosen as most fit to tell the mother, and smooth out matters as much as possible.

.   .   .   .

Pelageia Petrovna had just risen, and was preparing her morning tea when Ivan Golubenko, gloomy and confused, entered the room.

"Just in time for tea, Ivan Ivanovich!" amiably exclaimed the old lady, rising to meet her guest. "You have surely called to see Vladimir!"

"No, I—in passing by—" Golubenko stammered abashed.

"You will have to excuse him, he is still asleep. He walked up and down his room the whole of last night, and I told the servant not to wake him, as it is a—holy day. But probably you came on urgent business?"

"No, I only stepped in for a moment in passing—"

"If you wish to see him, I will give the order to wake him up."

"No, no, do not trouble yourself!"

But Pelageia Petrovna, believing that he had called to see her son on some business or other, left the room, murmuring to herself.

Golubenko walked excitedly to and fro, wringing his hands, not knowing how to tell her the terrible news. The decisive moment was quickly approaching, but he lost control of himself, was frightened, and cursed fate that had so mixed him up with the whole business.

"Now! How can a body trust you young people!" good-naturedly exclaimed Pelageia to her guest, reentering the room. "Here I have been taking care not to make the least noise with the cups and saucers, and asking you not to wake my boy, and he has long ago departed without leaving a trace! But why do you not take a seat, Ivan Ivanovich, and have a cup of tea? You have been neglecting us terribly lately!"

She smiled as with a secret joy, and added in a low voice:

"And we have had so much news during that

time!— Vladimir surely could not keep it. He must have told you all about it by this; for he is very straightforward and open-hearted, my Vladimir. I was thinking last night, in my sinful thoughts: 'Well, when my Vladimir paces the room the whole night—that means that he is dreaming of Lenochka!' That is always the case with him: if he paces the room the whole night, he will surely leave to-morrow— Ah, Ivan Ivanovich, I only ask the Lord to send me this joy in my old age. What more does an old woman need? I have but one desire, one joy— and it seems to me I shall have nothing more to pray for after Vladimir and Lenochka are married. So joyful and happy it would make me!— I do not need anything besides Vladimir; there is nothing dearer to me than his happiness."

The old lady became so affected that she had to wipe away the tears which came to her eyes.

"Do you remember," she continued, "things did not go well in the beginning—either between the two or on account of the money— You young officers are not even allowed to marry without bonds— Well, now everything has been arranged; I have obtained the necessary five thousand rubles for Vladimir, and they could go to the altar even to-morrow! Yes, and Lenochka has written such a lovely letter to me— My heart is rejoicing!"

Continuing to speak, Pelageia Petrovna took

a letter out of her pocket, which she showed to Golubenko, and then put back again.

"She is such a dear girl! And so good!"

Ivan Golubenko, listening to her talk, sat as if on red-hot coals. He wanted to interrupt her flow of words, to tell her that everything was at an end, that her Vladimir was dead, and that in one short hour nothing would remain to her of all her bright hopes; but he listened to her and kept silent. Looking upon her good, gentle face, he felt a convulsive gripping in his throat.

"But why are you looking so gloomy to-day?" the old lady at last asked. "Why, your face looks as black as night!"

Ivan wanted to say "Yes! And yours will be the same when I tell you!" but instead of telling her anything, he turned his head away, and began to twirl his mustaches.

Pelageia Petrovna did not notice it, and, wholly absorbed in her own thoughts, continued:

"I have a greeting for you. Lenochka writes that I should give Ivan Ivanovich her regards, and should compel him to come with Vladimir and pay her a visit— You know yourself how she likes you, Ivan Ivanovich!— No, it seems I am not able to keep it to myself. I must show you the letter. Just see for yourself how loving and sweet it is."

And Pelageia Petrovna again took out the package of letters from her pocket, took from it

a thin letter-sheet, closely written, and unfolded
it before Ivan Golubenko, whose face had become
still gloomier, and he tried to push away with
his hand the extended note, but Pelageia Petrovna had already started to read:

"DEAR PELAGEIA PETROVNA—When will the time arrive when I
will be able to address you, not as above, but as my dear, sweet
mother! I am anxiously awaiting the time, and hope so much that
it will soon come that even now I do not want to call you otherwise than mama—"

Pelageia Petrovna lifted her head, and, ceasing to read, looked at Golubenko with eyes suf-
fused with tears.

"You see, Ivan Ivanovich." she added; but seeing that Golubenko was biting his mustaches, and
that his eyes too were moist, she rose, placed a
trembling hand upon his hair, and quietly kissed
him on the forehead. "Thank you, Ivan Ivanovich," she whispered, greatly moved. "I always
thought that you and Vladimir were more like
brothers than like simple friends—Forgive me—
I am so very happy, God be thanked!"

Tears streamed down her cheeks, and Ivan
Golubenko was so disturbed and confused that
he could only catch in his own her cold, bony
hand and cover it with kisses; tears were suffocating him, and he could not utter a word, but in
this outburst of motherly love he felt such a terrible reproach to himself that he would have preferred to be lying himself upon the field, shot
through the head, than to hear himself praised
for his friendship by this woman who would in

half an hour find out the whole truth; what would she then think of him? Did not he, the friend, the almost brother, stand quietly by when a revolver was pointed at Vladimir? Did not this brother himself measure the space between the two antagonists and load the revolvers? All this he did himself, did consciously; and now this friend and brother silently sat there without having even the courage to fulfil his duty.

He was afraid; at this moment he despised himself, but could not prevail upon himself to say even one word. His soul was oppressed by a strange lack of harmony; he felt sick at heart and stifling. And in the meanwhile time flew— he knew it, and the more he knew it the less had he the courage to deprive Pelageia Petrovna of her few last happy moments. What should he say to her? How should he prepare her? Ivan Golubenko lost his head entirely.

He had had already time enough to curse in his thoughts all duels, all quarrels, every kind of heroism, and all kinds of so-called questions of honor, and he at last rose from his seat ready to confess or to run away. Silently and quickly he caught the hand of Pelageia Petrovna, and stooping over it to touch it with his lips, thus hid his face, over which a torrent of tears suddenly streamed down; impetuously, without another thought, he ran out into the corridor, snatching his great coat, and then out of the house without having said a word.

Pelageia Petrovna looked after him with astonishment, and thought:

"He also must be in love, poor fellow— Well, that is their young sorrow—before happiness!" . . .

And she soon forgot him, absorbed in her dreams of the happiness which seemed to her so inviolable and entire.

THE HANGING AT LA PIROCHE

BY ALEXANDRE DUMAS, FILS

THE HANGING AT LA PIROCHE

BY ALEXANDRE DUMAS, FILS

D O YOU know La Piroche?
No. No more do I. So I shall not
abuse my privilege as an author by giving you a description; especially since, between
you and me be it said, they are very tiresome,
those descriptions. Unless it be a question of
the virgin forests of America, as in Cooper, or of
Meschaccbé,[1] as in Chateaubriand, that is to say,
countries that are not close at hand, and about
which the imagination, to obtain a clear vision of
the details, must be assisted by those poetical
voyagers who have visited them, in general descriptions are not of much consequence except to
be skipped by the reader. Literature has this
advantage over painting, sculpture, and music;
the threefold advantage of being able to paint by
itself a picture in a single word, to carve a statue
in one phrase, to mold a melody on one page; it
must not abuse itself of that privilege, and one
should leave to the special arts a little of their
own prerogative. I own, then, for my part, and

[1] As the word "Mississippi" sounded to the French ear.

Translated by R. W. Howes, 3d. Copyright, 1907, by P. F. Collier & Son.

for lack of better advice, that when I find that I have to describe a country which every one has seen, or every one could see, if it be near, if it does not differ from our own, I prefer to leave to my reader the pleasure of recalling it if he has seen it, or of imagining it if he does not yet know it. The reader likes well enough to be left to do his share of the work he is reading. This flatters him and makes him believe that he is capable of doing the rest. Indeed, it is an excellent thing to flatter your reader. Moreover, the whole world in reality knows what the sea is like—a plain, a forest, a blue sky, an effect of sun, an effect of the moon, or an effect of storm. Of what use to dwell upon it? It would be far better to trace a landscape in one stroke of the brush like Rubens or Delacroix: this should be said without comparison and keep the whole value of your palette for the figures you wish to reanimate. When one blackens with descriptions page after page of paper, one doesn't give the reader an impression equal to that experienced by the most artless bourgeois who walks through the Bois de Vincennes on a soft April day, or by an unlettered girl who strolls in June, on the arm of her fiancé, at eleven o'clock at night through the shady vistas of the woods of Romainville or the park of Enghien. We all have in our minds and hearts a gallery of landscapes made from memory, and which serves as background for all the stories of the world. There is but one word to use—day or night, winter or spring, calm or storm, wood or plain—to evoke at once a most finished landscape. So I have only to tell you this: that at the moment when the story I am about to tell you begins it is noon, that it is May, that the highway we are going to enter is bordered on the right with furze bushes, on the left by the sea; you know at once all that I have not told you; that is to say, that the bushes are green, that the sea is murmuring, that the sky is blue, that the sun is warm, and that there is dust on the road.

I have only to add that this highway that winds along the coast of Brittany runs from La Poterie to La Piroche; that Piroche is a village about which I know nothing, but which must be more or less like all villages, that we are in the middle of the fifteenth century, in 1418, and that two men, one older than the other, one the father of the other, both peasants, are following the highway mounted on two nags trotting along comfortably enough for two nags under the weight of two peasants.

"Shall we get there in time?" said the son.

"Yes, it is not to take place until two o'clock," replied the father, "and the sun marks but a quarter after noon."

"Oh, but I am curious to see that!"

"I can well believe it."

"So he will be hanged in the armor that he stole?"

"Yes."

"How the devil did he get the idea of stealing armor?"

"It's not the idea that is hard to get—"

"It's the armor," interrupted the boy, who wanted his share in making a part of that joke.

"And that, too, he didn't get."

"Was it fine armor?"

"Splendid, they say, all shining with gold."

"And did they catch him as he was carrying it away?"

"Yes, you know as well as I do that armor like that never goes astray without raising a great outcry; it can't escape its proper owner all by itself."

"So, then, it was of iron?"

"They woke up in the château at the noise they heard."

"And did they arrest the man?"

"Not at once; they began by being afraid."

"Of course, it's always that way that people who have been robbed begin when they are in the presence of thieves; otherwise there would be no object in being a thief."

"No, nor any pleasant excitement in being robbed! But those brave folks had no idea that it was an affair of robbery."

"Of what, then?"

"Of a ghost. That wretched, most vigorous fellow was carrying the armor in front of him, holding his head at the height of the loins of said armor so effectively that he acquired gigantic proportions in the corridor where he passed. Add to this a clattering noise which the rascal made behind him, and you will appreciate the fright of the valets. But, unfortunately for him, he woke up the Seigneur of La Piroche, he who has fear of neither the dead nor the living, who easily, and all by himself, arrested the thief and handed him over, bound, to his well-deserved justice."

"And his well-deserved justice?"

"The condemned man is to be hanged clothed in the armor."

"Why that clause in the sentence?"

"Because the Seigneur of La Piroche is not only a brave captain, but a man of common sense and of spirit, who wished to draw from this just condemnation an example for others and an advantage for himself. Why, don't you know that whatever touches a hanged man becomes a talisman for him who possesses it? So the Seigneur of La Piroche has ordered that the thief should be hanged dressed in his armor, so as to reclaim it when the man is dead and have a talisman to wear during our next wars."

"That is very ingenious."

"I should think so."

"Let's make haste, for I am so anxious to see the poor man hanged."

"We have plenty of time! We must not wear our beasts out. We are not going to stop at La Piroche; we will have to go on a league farther, and then return to La Poterie."

"Yes, but our beasts will rest for five or six hours, for we do not return until evening."

The father and son continued on their way, talking, and half an hour later they reached La Piroche.

As the father had said, they arrived on time. Have fathers always the privilege of being right?

There was an immense concourse of people on the great square in front of the château, for it was there that the scaffold had been erected, a splendid gallows, in faith, of sound oak, not very high, it is true, since it was intended for a wretched, obscure criminal, but high enough, nevertheless, for death to do its work between earth and the end of the rope which was swinging in the fresh sea breeze like an eel hanging by its tail.

The condemned man was certain of having a beautiful view at the moment of death, for he was to die with his face turned toward the ocean. If this view could be any consolation to him, so much the better, but, for my part, I doubt it.

And all the while the sea was blue, and from time to time between the azure of the sky and that of the sea floated a white cloud, like an angel on its way to heaven, but whose long robes still trailed upon the earth it was quitting.

The two companions approached as near as possible to the scaffold, so as to miss nothing that was going on, and, like all the rest, they waited, having this advantage over the others, that they were mounted on two nags and could see better with less fatigue.

They had not long to wait.

At a quarter of two the gates of the château opened, and the condemned man appeared, preceded by the guards of the Seigneur of La Piroche and followed by the executioner.

The thief was dressed in the stolen armor and was mounted reversed on the bare back of a jackass. He rode with vizor down and head lowered. They had tied his hands behind his back, and if they wish for our opinion in the matter we have no hesitation in saying that, judging by his position, in default of his face, which could not be seen, he ought to have been very ill at ease, and indulging at that moment in very sad reflections.

They conducted him to the side of the scaffold, and a moving picture hardly pleasant for him began to silhouette itself against the blue sky. The hangman set his ladder against the scaffold, and the chaplain of the Seigneur of La Piroche, mounted on a prepared platform, delivered the sentence of justice.

The condemned man did not move. One might have said that he had given the spectators the slip by dying before he was hanged.

They called to him to descend from his ass and deliver himself to the hangman.

He did not move. We understand his hesitation.

Then the hangman took him by the elbows,

lifted him off the ass, and set him upright on the ground.

Fine fellow, that hangman!

When we say that he set him upright, we do not lie. But we would lie in saying that he remained as they placed him. He had in two minutes jumped two-thirds of the alphabet; that is to say, in vulgar parlance, that instead of standing straight like an I, he became zigzag like a Z.

During this time the chaplain finished reading the sentence.

"Have you any request to make?" he asked of the culprit.

"Yes," replied the unfortunate, in a voice sad and low.

"What do you ask?"

"I ask for pardon."

I do not know if the word "farceur" was invented in those days, but then or never was the time to invent it and to speak it.

The Seigneur of La Piroche shrugged his shoulders and ordered the executioner to do his duty.

The latter made ready to mount the ladder leaning against the gibbet, which, impassive, was about to draw with extended arm the soul out of a body, and he attempted to make the condemned mount in front of him, but it was not an easy thing to do. One does not know, in general, what obstacles those condemned to death will put in the way of their dying.

THE HANGING AT LA PIROCHE

The hangman and the man there had the air of passing civilities one to another. It was a question of who should go first.

The hangman, to make him mount on his ladder, returned to the method he employed in making him descend from his ass. He seized him around the middle of his body, balanced him on the third rung of the ladder, and began to push him up from beneath.

"Bravo!" cried the crowd.

He ought to have mounted well.

Then the executioner adroitly slipped the running noose, which adorned the end of the rope, around the neck of the culprit, and, giving the latter a vigorous kick in the back, he flung him out into space, which strongly resembled Eternity.

An immense clamor greeted this looked-for dénouement, and a shudder passed through the crowd. Whatever may be the crime he has committed, the man who dies is always at the moment greater than those who watch him die.

The hanged man swung for three or four minutes at the end of his rope, as he had a right to do, danced, wriggled, then hung motionless and rigid.

The Z had become an I again.

They gazed a while longer on the culprit, whose gilded armor glistened in the sun, then the spectators divided themselves, little by little, into groups, and went their way home, chatting about the event.

"Pooh! a horrid thing is death!" said the son of the peasant, as he continued his journey with his father.

"In good faith, to hang one for not having succeeded in stealing a piece of armor, that's expensive. What do you think?"

"I wonder, I do, what they would have done to him if he had really stolen the armor?"

"They would not have done anything to him, for if he had really stolen the armor he would have been able to escape from the château. Then, possibly, he would not have returned to be arrested."

"Yet he is punished more for a crime that he has not committed than he would have been if he had committed the crime!"

"But he had the intention of committing it."

"And the intention was accounted as a fact—"

"That is perfectly just."

"But it isn't pretty to look at."

And since they found themselves on rising ground, the two companions turned to contemplate for the last time the silhouette of the unfortunate.

Twenty minutes later they entered the little town where, save the mark! they were to receive certain moneys, and which they were to leave that evening in order to accomplish the return home that same night.

On the morrow, at break of day, the guards sallied out from the château of La Piroche for the

purpose of taking down the corpse of the hanging man, from which they intended to recover the
armor of the Seigneur, but they discovered something which they had been far from anticipating,
that is to say, the gibbet was there, as always, but
the hanged man was not there.

The two guards rubbed their eyes, believing
themselves to be dreaming, but the thing was very
real. No more hanged man, and naturally no
more armor.

And what was extraordinary, the rope was
neither broken nor cut, but just in the condition
it was before receiving the condemned.

The two guards ran to announce this news to
the Seigneur of La Piroche. He was not willing
to believe it, and proceeded to assure himself of
the truth of the facts. So puissant a seigneur
was he that he was convinced the hanged man
would reappear for him there; but he saw what
all the rest had seen.

What had become of the dead? For the condemned had certainly died the day before, before
the eyes of the whole village.

Had another thief profited by the night to get
possession of the armor that covered the corpse?

Possibly—but in taking the armor he would
naturally leave the corpse, for which he had no
use.

Had the friends or relations of the culprit
wished to give him Christian burial?

Nothing impossible in that if it were not for the

fact that the culprit had neither friends nor relations, and that people who had had religious
sentiments like that would have taken the culprit
and left the armor. That, then, was no longer to
be thought of. What should one believe, then?

The Seigneur of La Piroche was in despair.
He was all for his armor. He made promise of a
reward of ten gold *écus* to any one who should
deliver to him the thief, dressed as he was in
dying.

They ransacked the houses; they found nothing.

No one presented himself.

They caused a sage of the town of Rennes to
be sent for, and they propounded this question to
him:

"In what way does a dead man who has been
hanged manage to free himself from the rope that
holds him in the air by the neck?"

The sage demanded eight days to ponder over
the question, at the termination of which he replied:

"He can not do it."

Then they propounded this second question:

"A thief, unsuccessful in stealing while alive,
and having been condemned to death for stealing,
can he steal after his death?"

The sage replied:

"Yes."

He was asked how it could be done. He replied that he knew nothing about it.

THE HANGING AT LA PIROCHE

He was the greatest sage of his time.

They sent him home and contented themselves with believing, for those were the days of witchcraft, that the thief was a wizard.

Then they said masses to exorcise that evil spirit, which was without doubt taking his revenge upon the Seigneur who had ordered his death and upon those who had come to see him die.

A month passed in fruitless search.

The gibbet still stood there as always, humiliated, gloomy, and discredited. Never had a gibbet committed such a breach of confidence.

The Seigneur of La Piroche continued to clamor for his armor from man, God, and the devil.

Nothing.

At last he was beginning, without a doubt, to make the best of this strange event, and of the loss which had been the result, when one morning, as he was waking, he heard a great commotion on the square where the execution had taken place. He was making ready to inform himself of what was passing when his chaplain entered the room.

"Monseigneur," said he, "do you know what has happened?"

"No, but I am going to ask."

"I can tell you, I can."

"What is it, then?"

"A miracle from heaven!"

"Really!"

"The hanged man—"

"Well?"

"He is there!"

"Where?"

"On the scaffold."

"Hanging?"

"Yes, Monseigneur."

"In his armor?"

"In your armor."

"True, for it *is* mine. And is he dead?"

"Absolutely dead—only—"

"Only what?"

"Did he have spurs on when they hanged him?"

"No."

"Well, Monseigneur, he has them, and in place of having the casque on his head, he has placed it with great care at the foot of the gibbet, and left his head hanging uncovered."

"Let us see, Mr. Chaplain, let us see, straight off!"

The Seigneur of La Piroche ran to the square crowded with the curious. The neck of the hanged man had passed again into the running noose, the corpse was there at the end of the rope, and the armor was there on the corpse.

It was astounding. So they proclaimed it a miracle.

"He has repented," said one, "and has come to hang himself over again."

THE HANGING AT LA PIROCHE

"He has been there all the time," said another; "only we did not see him."

"But why has he got spurs?" asked a third.

"No doubt, because he has come from afar and wished to return in a hurry."

"I know well, for my part, that far or near, I would not have needed to put on spurs, for I would not have come back."

And they laughed, and they stared at the ugly face the dead man made.

As for the Seigneur of La Piroche, he thought of nothing but of making sure that the thief was quite dead, and of securing his armor.

They cut down the corpse and stripped it; then, once despoiled, they hung it up again, and the ravens investigated so thoroughly that at the end of two days it was all jagged, at the end of eight days it had only the appearance of a rag, and at the end of fifteen days it had no longer the appearance of anything at all; or, if it did resemble anything, it was only those impossible hanged men we used to make pictures of on the first page of our text-book, and below which we wrote the amphibious quatrain, half Latin, half French:

Aspice Pierrot pendu,
Qui nunc librum n'a pas rendu,
Si hunc librum reddidisset:
Pierrot pendu *non-faisset.*[2]

[2] Behold Pierrot suspendered,
Who has not his Latin rendered.
But 'twas otherwisely fated:
Pierrot was the one translated.

But what had the hanged man been doing during his month of absence? How did it happen that he escaped, and, having escaped, that he hanged himself again?

We will give below the three versions which have been presented to us.

A magician, a pupil of Merlin, declared that if at the moment of dying the culprit has had the will to disappear and the ability to absorb his body into his will, the will being an immaterial thing, invisible, and impalpable, the body, which finds itself absorbed by it, and consequently hidden in it, becomes by that means also impalpable, immaterial, and invisible, and that if the body of a thief has reappeared at the end of a month, and at the end of a rope, it is because at that supreme moment his will, troubled by his conscience, has not had sufficient force for eternal absorption.

This may not be a good version, but it is one.

The theologians affirm that the culprit did succeed in vanishing, but that, pursued by remorse and being in haste to reconcile himself with God, he could not endure the life longer than one month, and, full of repentance, came to execute upon himself that justice which he had escaped the first time.

That, perhaps, is not the true version, but it is always Christian logic, and as a Christian we will not dismiss it altogether.

Finally, they declared that our two peasants in returning home that evening, and passing close

to the gibbet, heard lamentations, a rattling, and
something like a prayer; that they piously crossed
themselves and demanded what was the matter;
that they received no reply, but the lamentations
continued, and it seemed to them that they came
from the corpse that was above their heads. Then
they took the ladder that the hangman had left at
the foot of the scaffold, rested it against the arm
of the gibbet, and the son, having mounted to the
level of the condemned, said to him:

"Is it you who are making these complaints,
poor man?"

The condemned gathered all his strength together and said:

"Yes."

"Then you are still alive?"

"Yes."

"You repent of your crime?"

"Yes."

"Then I will loosen you, and since the Evan-
gelist commands us to give succor to those who
suffer, and that you suffer, I am going to succor
you and bring you to life in order to bring you
to good. God prefers a soul that repents to a
corpse that expiates."

Then the father and the son cut down the
dying man, and saw how it was that he still lived.
The rope, instead of tightening about the neck of
the thief, had tightened at the base of the casque
so effectually that the culprit was suspended but
not strangled, and, occupying with his head a kind

of vantage-point in the interior of the casque, he was able to breathe and to keep alive up to the time our two companions passed by.

The latter took him down and carried him home with them, where they gave him into the care of the mother and the young daughter.

But he who has stolen will steal.

There were but two things to steal at the peasant's, for the money he had brought back with him was not in his house. These two things were his horse and his daughter, a fair-haired girl of sixteen.

The ex-hanged decided to steal both the one and the other, for he was covetous of the horse and had fallen in love with the daughter.

So one night he saddled the horse, buckled on the spurs to make him ride faster, and went to take the young girl while she was asleep, and lift her up on to the crupper.

But the girl awoke and cried out.

The father and the son came running up. The thief tried to escape, but he was too late. The young girl told about the attempt of the hanged man; and the father and the son, seeing well that no repentance was to be expected from such a man, resolved to execute justice upon him, but more effectually than the Seigneur of La Piroche had allowed himself to do it. They bound the thief to the horse which he had saddled himself, led him to the square of La Piroche, and strung him up there where he had been hanged, but placed his casque on the ground to make sure that he should not vanish again; then they returned home quietly.

There is the third version. I do not know why I believe it to be the most probable, and that you would do well, like me, to give it preference over the other two.

As for the Seigneur of La Piroche, as soon as he had secured a real talisman, he went happily off to the wars, where he was the first to be killed.

THE GRAY NUN

BY NATALY VON ESCHSTRUTH

THE GRAY NUN

BY NATALY VON ESCHSTRUTH

W HEN I was a young man I once made a foreign journey, betaking myself to the royal court of X. on affairs of state. In those days politics would take strange turns, not of unmixed delight, and so it happened that my mission was prolonged well into the winter, and kept me at X. until the carnival season. But at this I did not repine, for to pass a winter in a beautiful climate and amid the fascinating society of a court seemed a welcome change to my enthusiastic, pleasure-loving young soul.

The reigning sovereign had a predilection for masked balls,—a traditionally favorite amusement at the palace, I was told—and accordingly several fancy dress festivities were enacted on the royal premises during the carnival. The first I was unable to participate in because of an inflamed eye, and therefore awaited the second with all the keener anticipation.

In the becoming costume of a Prussian officer in the army of Frederick the Great, and with the agreeable sensation of being specially well disguised beneath my mask and safe from recogni-

Translated by Lionel Strachey, from the German, for Short Stories.

tion, I mingled in the gay throng of the dancers and enjoyed to the full the charm of the brilliant and delicious event. An exquisitely graceful little water-nix had conquered my heart. The champagne was bubbling in my blood, and in wild spirits I was pursuing the fleeing Undine into an adjacent apartment.

Suddenly I stopped as though spellbound, and found myself staring into a pair of dark eyes, black as night, which were rigidly fixed upon me. Standing aloof, in a corner of the room, I saw a nun. Her long gray garment reached to the ground, and lay about her very feet in folds like a train. Her arms hung straight down, the hands being concealed in the loose sleeves. White linen bands covered her head and chin, and rendered even her mouth invisible, while her forehead and the upper part of her face were protected by a black velvet mask. And the blackness of those eyes that penetrated me was so intense that scarcely were any whites discernible.

An indescribable emotion ran over me as I stood under the ban of an evil power, as it were, returning the look of that strange figure. I had forgotten Undine. Drawn by some invisible force, I approached the nun with mechanical footstep.

"Why, fair mask," I accosted her with a bold laugh, "are you alone? Surely you know that for dancing and love two are needed!"

Briefly, like a Chinese idol, she nodded her head in assent; a thrill seemed to pass over her wonderfully slender shape; yet she did not budge.

I became more venturesome from a sudden feeling as of fire rushing through my veins.

"You may be vowed to seclusion, beautiful bride of Heaven, but to-day the convent walls have released you, to-day you are of the world and the flesh, to-day you are mine!"

Thus I cried aloud, forgetting in my excitement that I was in a country where my mother tongue was only spoken and understood at the German legation.

In a moment it occurred to me: Did the mask know German?

To my astonishment, she gave an immediate sign of intelligence by gliding, silently as a shadow, another step in my direction, and her blazing eyes appeared to kindle with merriment. Had she a veil over her eyes? It almost looked so, and this extraordinary measure of precaution challenged me the more strongly to overcome her reluctance to being known.

"Do you understand me?" I asked.

She nodded in the same brief, jerky manner as before.

"Do you know me?"

Similarly she answered by negative motions of the head. I stepped up close to her with the question:

"But will you not know me and love me? Come into my arms, and let us dance!"

Then something happened that at the moment I found surprising and extremely startling, yet which I took for a mere carnival freak, while later on I could scarce review the occurrence with any degree of clearness.

The nun threw her arms about me abruptly and almost desperately, and whirled me into a frenzied dance. I felt no body between my arms, and did not hear the rustle of her dress; I only saw those enigmatic dark eyes, which glowed near, very near, my own. And in mad career, regardless of the musical time or of the tune played, my curious partner tore around the room with me faster and faster, and with ever increasing fury. Her arms gripped me tighter and tighter and I was threatened with complete loss of breath in the wild race. Of a sudden I received a violent blow, resembling an electric shock, from each of her hands on my shoulders, felt myself all at once liberated, and staggered faint against a pyramid of plants. Boisterous laughter sounded on my ear; some other masks had surrounded and seized me, exclaiming:

"Look at the fine gentleman! He is out of his mind, dancing about the room like a madman, quite alone!"

I opened my eyes and looked all around. What had become of my partner?

Not a sign of her was to be seen, although this

other room was likewise very large, just then not well filled with people.

"Have I been dancing alone?" I gasped, tearing the mask off my burning face.

"Quite alone! Did you imagine it was with your sweetheart?" was the mocking, noisy reply.

I was deeply annoyed. "Nonsense!" I cried. "You are all in the conspiracy! Where has the nun gone? It was no lady at all, it was a man in disguise!"

They laughed still more, and some whispered behind fans that I must be drunk.

Strange sensations invaded me. Had a joke been played at my expense? Had a member of the German legation dressed in female clothes, and in the height of his whimsical caprice danced with me in that insane fashion? Were the guests in the secret, and were they amusing themselves—as the freedom of the carnival permitted—with teasing a foreigner? Yet surely the mysterious nun must be discoverable. My knees were trembling from a weakness I was unable to account for, but I collected myself, and while various thoughts coursed through my brain for a solution of this carnival prank, I hastened with feverish speed through rooms and galleries in quest of the nun. But in vain. I espied neither herself, nor met anyone who had seen her. The lackeys and doorkeepers assured me in perfect good faith that they had seen no nun of any sort.

"The costume is one of which His Majesty

does not approve," I was informed in the cloak-
room. "It is considered irreverent to appear at
balls here in the spiritual garb of a nun or a
monk, and therefore it is not done. It would
certainly have been observed by us had any lady
or gentleman transgressed against the prevail-
ing usage."

"Then perhaps I may have mistaken for a nun
some other mask, who intended in her gray suit
to represent Twilight or Care," I excused myself
hesitatingly, though I had an accurate eye for
dresses, and could have registered a solemn oath
that the mysterious unknown was even wearing
especially authentic claustral attire. No one,
however, could by any effort remember having
noticed a costume anything like that described
by me.

"Are there any secret passages to any of the
rooms and galleries which are the scene of to-
night's festivities?" I asked a doorkeeper. He
looked at me in surprise, and answered:

"All ways of communication were opened to-
day because of the crowd of guests, but for
safety's sake guarded and watched more carefully than usual. Only the tapestried corridor
running the length of the great colonnade to the
royal apartments was left unguarded, since in
that place there is no possibility of improper in-
trusion."

A new idea flashed across me. The spot on
which I had first set eyes on my nun was at the

entrance to that corridor. Might not a member
of the royal family have elected to make me, as
a novice in this foreign court society, the subject
of a merry jest? No doubt the nun was a man in
disguise, and the young princes and dukes were
probably capable of pouncing on the victim and
dancing him to death.

My confusion was perhaps very diverting, and
the secrecy of the few spectators of the joke,
who were, of course, initiated, was quite praise-
worthy. They asserted not having seen a nun at
all, and laughed at me for having rushed round
the room alone, like a lunatic. Obviously there
was no further room for doubt, this explanation
and no other was valid. Why had I not thought
of this before!

So I joined in the hilarity of the others and
made the best of my discomfiture. In any case,
the manner in which my partner had dismissed
me betrayed a pair of powerful masculine fists!
My shoulders, on which she had come down so
vigorously, ached as if they were broken, and I
was still unable to conquer entirely a peculiar
sensation of uneasiness. But while I was pursuing my investigations the clock struck twelve,
the company unmasked, and gaily flocked toward the supper rooms. I felt particularly en-
titled to refreshments, and in the course of my
indulgence in the good things of my selection,
my faintness—which was more astonishing to my
robust, muscular young self than any carnival

joke in the world could have been—passed off
completely. I was as happy and lively as before,
and enjoyed the remainder of the ball as much
as I had the beginning. I tried to dismiss the
episode from my mind. For a few days I felt
a dull pain in my shoulders, which annoyed me
at night also, and disturbed my sleep. The image
of the nun haunted me, and the sombre, penetrating eyes were present to me in my very
dreams. This vexed me, and I mentally abused
the royal gentleman in every key who had pushed
his joke rather too far.

A week passed, and the court chamberlain
issued invitations for the third masked ball at the
palace. I purchased a sailor's dress, and on the
evening of the ball tripped up the marble stairs
in the best of spirits. It had in the meanwhile
occurred to me that I had perhaps imbibed too
much, and that the prince in nun's clothing had
perhaps observed my condition, and made me his
victim for that reason. But I rejected that
proposition. In the first place, I had not taken
much to drink; certainly two or three glasses of
champagne and lemonade were not worth men-
tioning when I remembered what quantities of
alcohol I had frequently absorbed in my university days in Germany. I was a brave boon
companion, and capable of consuming a great
deal. So how should a few paltry little glasses
make me so unsteady on my feet as to collapse
in dancing a fast gallop? Absurd! I was sure

enough of myself, and sufficiently well brought up in social customs, to know how much one may drink at a court ball. No—I was convinced that I had not been intoxicated, but on this occasion I resolved to exercise special caution, and to be strictly temperate, in the event of the disguised perpetrator of pranks again attempting to make the German stranger the butt of his impudence. This time he should meet his match; I would keep my head clear and my feet steady enough to venture a dance with him. The constantly suspicious attitude of my mind, to be sure, interfered with my pleasure very considerably. I was in a too observant mood to float on the topmost wave of enjoyment, and besides an extraordinary disquietude had seized upon me, a contraction about the heart that was quite new to me, such as sensitive people undergo before a storm or in anticipation of momentous changes of fortune. I wandered about restlessly. Numerous though the merry masks that flitted around me, that nun's indescribable black eyes did not appear, and no effort was made to involve me again as the hero of another frolic. Time was dragging heavily. I glanced at my watch, and wished the supper hour might be near. The finger only pointed to half past eleven, so that I must still possess my soul in patience for half an hour. It was a lovely, mild, moonlight night; the doors to the tapestried passage and the colonnade had been thrown open, and I concluded to take a breath of the fragrant air and a rapid view of the illuminated town in its festive brilliancy of a carnival night.

A female pierrot dances past me with Don Juan, and, with a laugh, throws a handful of confetti in my face. I retaliate—a few phrases are exchanged—I look after her for a moment— and then turn to the entrance of the corridor, to get out into the colonnade.

I am rooted to the ground!

Standing aside in a corner, on the very same spot as before, is my nun, staring at me with the same unfathomable eyes as a week ago!

Where had she come from?

Out of the ground? Or had she slipped in through the door during my banter with the pierrot?

She had come through the door, of course.

I am utterly amazed. The same costume. The same joke. How clumsy of the prince to repeat himself. I am inclined to ignore the impertinent young gentleman, and pass him proudly by—yet—strange—again I am attracted irresistibly, as by a supernatural power, held by those black orbs. I am quite certain of my wits this time: the dress is really the forbidden costume of a nun, and, so far as I can judge, exact in every particular. On her breast hangs a large cross, which is especially conspicuous. It is of dull gold, with emeralds and pearls inlaid, of

peculiar shape, and certainly antique. The pious
nun seems to have regaled herself with excessive
haste at some sideboard, since the white collar
and the front of the gray bodice show oblong
dark stains, as though some beverage had been
spilt.

"Well, fair mask," I finally remark in a mocking tone, although my heart is beating furiously,
"you have been waiting for me here, I presume?"

She nods slowly and solemnly.

"Do you imagine, by chance, that I wish to
dance another hurricane with you?"

Again she assents, but more emphatically.

"Then," say I, ironically, "see where you can
find a new blockhead, my muscular fairy! My
shoulders are not well yet!"

Her arms move—hands there are none visible
in the long, roomy sleeves—they are stretched
out to me as if in mute appeal. A cold shiver
runs down my back, I know not why.

"If I dance with you again," I angrily exclaim, "you will not fare quite so well as last
time! I am firmer on my feet to-night than I
was last week!"

She presses her arms to her breast, something
like a tremor agitates the gray shape, and her
head is slightly raised. Her position and demeanor, though she utters not a word, denote
intense longing.

The blood rushes to my head—I must go a step
nearer to her—I must!

"If I dance with you, it will be only on one condition!"

With a profound sigh her bosom heaves, her arms fall to her side, her body is humbly bent forward as if in complete surrender, and as if to say: Ask what you will!

"My condition is that you afterward reveal yourself."

She nods stiffly, like a marionette.

"Swear to it!"

She raises her arm for the oath, but the gray folds still conceal her hand.

"Woe betide you if you deceive me!"

She shakes her head, and repeats the passionate gesture of entreaty. Her slender form trembles with feverish impatience, and the wonderful eyes seem to plead, in extreme urgency: Come quickly!

I put out my arms—

Once more does the terrible woman rush at me, once more am I held in that mad embrace, once more—on the wings of the wind—do we dash round the room! And once more are all my senses lost in the fiendish whirl!

I attempt to struggle, would pit the abounding strength of my youth against the woman and subdue her. In vain! I can think, I can act, no longer. My whole being is in a swoon, and I am conscious of nothing but two icy lips pressed upon mine with a vehemence calculated to draw my very life out of me.

A shudder seizes me, and the fear of death, and then—again that blow on my shoulders—

I feel as if a pair of iron clamps had been taken off me and I had been freed, and I sink down upon a sofa.

A laughing, jeering crowd surrounds me, shouting:

"The sailor is crazy! He has gone out of his mind!"

Have I again been dancing alone in public?

I jump up in a rage, and exclaim, as I toss back my dishevelled hair from my burning brow:

"Abominable trickery! Let me pass! Let me get my hands on her, and unmask her!"

Something rings on the floor. It has fallen from my hand, hitherto clenched and just now opened. Triumphantly I snatch it up, exulting:

"Her cross! Ha! that shall be my clue!"

On this occasion, too, no trace of the mysterious nun was to be found. It was at first superciliously assumed, as before, that I must be drunk or insane, but my serious mood and energetic investigations soon altered that notion. I might myself have doubted my mental soundness had it not been for the cross in my hand, which I at once recognized as being that worn by the nun, and had not a lackey finally confessed to having beheld the strange figure. He was coming from the colonnade with a tray of refreshments when he saw me in conversation with her. The mask had something familiar about her, he said, but he could not remember where he had seen her before. He had been a servant in the palace for forty years.

Nobody thought of a spectre; on the other hand extravagant speculations became rife of a conspirator being at work. It was rumored the king had originally intended to wear a sailor costume. Of course, it was him the uncanny visitor had designs upon. In view of the fact that the political horizon was very dark and clouded at that time, the conjecture was perhaps not altogether phantastical, and for this reason the report quickly reached the ears of the king and the royal family. I was promptly summoned before His Majesty, and it gave me a sort of revengeful pleasure to relate the incident to that august person. For I was still fully persuaded that some young member of his family had played this obnoxious trick upon me.

The king nodded thoughtfully upon my frank declaration that, according to my researches, the enigmatical female could only have come from the royal apartments.

Said his Majesty:

"May I ask you, my dear Baron, to show me the cross you found?"

I put it into his hand.

For a moment the king stared upon it speechless. Then he turned it over, and ejaculated, roughly almost under the emotion of his violent surprise:

"Great God—why—it is—!"

And he pointed to the small, delicately engraved initials, surmounted by a crown, in the middle of the cross. Very pale and with heaving breast he went on:

"A nun, a gray nun, you say? What would the object of such a joke be? and how—how should this cross come back among the living? Baron, come with me, I must request your confidence and secrecy!"

We passed through several rooms, and then arrived at a narrow gallery whose walls were hung with portraits of royal personages. The king came abruptly to a halt, and without himself looking up indicated a certain picture:

"Observe that painting! Do you see the same cross there that you have in your hand?"

Involuntarily I uttered the loud cry:

"Why, that is she! Holy Heavens! It is my nun!"

"The cross—compare the cross!" urged the king, his slender, white hand trembling with agitation.

A frosty current ran through my veins as I compared the pictured cross with that in my companion's hand. It was the same—not a doubt of it—and the eyes, too, were the same, as also the dress and the whole figure were unmistakably those of the gray nun I had danced with. Yet in those conspicuously large, deep black eyes lay not an expression of peacefulness and mild resignation, but a world of passionate feeling. Having assured the king of the identity of the cross, and he having informed me that it was an ancient heirloom of which no duplicate existed, he bade me accompany him further.

Arrived in the antechamber to his apartments, the king gave an order to one of the attendants on duty there. He walked up and down the room for a few moments in visible excitement, and then, stopping before me, and looking at me searchingly, he asked:

"Have you ever, in the course of your life, met with a manifestation of the supernatural?"

I was so bewildered and nervous that I scarcely could remember enough French to reply:

"May it please your Majesty, I have not."

"Do you believe in the possibility of the dead returning?"

"Not in the sense of their coming as apparitions. I always was, still am, a skeptic on the point of ghost stories in general, nevertheless I am a Christian, and I believe and know that we continue to live after death."

The king stared at me mechanically:

"You are a Protestant, and you say you are a skeptic. Curious—only you saw the apparition —it was revealed to no one else?"

"Then your Majesty is of the opinion that this is actually a case of a spectral apparition?"

"Certainly. It seems much more plausible than open theft. This very cross I myself—"

He interrupted his sentence as he turned to the door, through which, with profound obeisances, entered two ladies in waiting—probably the queen's. His Majesty addressed one of them in French, no doubt to enable me to participate in the conversation:

"You were present, Madame M., when Princess A. was laid in her coffin seventeen years ago?"

A low curtsey was the affirmative reply.

"And you also, Madame U.?"

"I had the honor, your Majesty, of rendering her royal highness the last earthly services."

"You remember perfectly what dress the deceased was buried in?"

"Quite well, your Majesty. It was the regular dress of the Order of Gray Sisters, of which her royal highness was a member."

"Do you recollect whether she took any ornaments to her last resting place?"

"Excepting the golden cross which your Majesty hung round her neck on the day she took the vow, no jewelry was put on the princess. The duchess even drew the little sapphire ring from her royal highness' finger, to keep it as a remembrance and wear it herself."

"You are absolutely certain that the cross went into the coffin? You could swear to it?"

"I could do so with fullest conviction, your Majesty."

"Would you recognize the cross?"

"To be sure I should."

"Is this it?"

"Good Heavens—it is! On the back there ought to be the initials of her royal highness!"

"Here they are," said the king, reversing the cross. The old woman shrank back appalled.

"Then, your Majesty, the vault has been broken into!"

"Possibly it has. The matter shall be investigated. I am much obliged to you, ladies, and earnestly request you will both preserve unconditional silence as to our present interview."

"Well," said the king to me, after the ladies in waiting had withdrawn, "how do you account for this cross being here in my hand, considering it was put into the coffin? You think the vault may have been pillaged? That, I believe, is out of the question. The object of a carnival freak, which could have been perpetrated just as easily in any other dress, is far too slight to make such a horrible offense as the violation of the dead worth while! But I intend to have the vault examined, and beg, my dear baron, that you will attend. For the present, good night."

I spent a dreadful night, torturing my sleepless brain for a solution of the riddle, and being forever haunted by the nun's dark eyes. It was late when I woke.

Some hours after, the coffin was opened in the presence of the king, whose surmise proved correct. The bolts on the coffin were intact. The gold chain was there, safe round the princess' neck. But the cross was gone. There was not the remotest sign of violence.

How I got out of that vault, I do not know. I remember feeling faint, and being supported by two court officials. I am unaware of what happened next. It was the only instance in my life in which my system had so entirely given way. A serious illness was apprehended, but my strong constitution won the day. For a long time my mind was in a precarious state.

When I had recovered, the king sent for me.

"Are you still a skeptic?" he asked in a grave voice.

"No, your Majesty, I am convinced now."

Whereupon the king himself deigned to communicate to me the particulars relating to the golden cross.

Princess A. was a daughter of one of his cousins, and she was their fifth child. The duchess, a very pious woman, made a vow before the birth of her sixth child, that if it was a boy, her youngest daughter should be dedicated to the service of the church and take the veil. A son was born, and Princess A. henceforth was educated for the profession of a nun in becoming retirement and seclusion. Unfortunately, however, the natural traits of the girl seemed to be entirely in oppositon to that reverend calling. An irrepressible vivacity of spirit, an intense coveting of worldly joys and pleasures characterized her, and the more she was separated from the world the more ardent grew her desire to live in it. Heartrending scenes of resistance and tears were enacted, and the reigning sovereign felt so much pity for the spirited young creature that he attempted to save her from her fate of being immured in convent walls by offering to apply to the pope for a dispensation releasing the mother from her promise. But the duchess desperately combated this idea. Her wild laments, that to break her vow would entail her forfeiture of eternal salvation, her protestations, her tears, her entreaties, at last prevailed upon the princess to join the Order of the Gray Sisters. For a short space all seemed to go well. The fervid heart of the royal nun was apparently beating placidly, in the quiet claustral surroundings. But during the winter the duchess fell sick, and the young bride of the church was called to her bedside. Princess A. had remained with her mother for several weeks, and about that time the carnival season began. Masked balls were given in the palace, and while the horns and violins were sounding in the ballroom Princess A. lay on her knees in the throes of dreadful despair, tearing her hair in furious longing for that lost paradise. She at last succeeded in bribing a chambermaid to secretly procure her a fancy dress. If it was to cost her immortal soul, once she would dance and be young and happy! The plot was betrayed, and the angriest reproaches were poured out by her parents upon the perjured, rebellious nun! Princess A. was locked up, and was to be removed to the convent the next day. However, as the festivities in the palace were reaching their height that night, the unhappy young nun lay expiring in her room. She had taken poison, although the report was spread in the capital that failure of the heart had caused her death. How she came into possession of the poison no one ever discovered. While she was writhing in terrible agony her half-crazed mother put a cup of milk to her lips as an antidote. She dashed it passionately aside and the spilt milk left stains on her dress.

How hard it was to die! Again and again she tore her black hair. Again and again she uttered the bitterest imprecations and the fiercest cries for a taste of youth and happiness. At length she stood up, straining her ears for the music in the ballroom.

And then she screamed aloud:

"Oh, I must dance once! I must kiss once! Let me be happy once! I cannot die before I dance! Let me go—let me dance—let me—"

She drew herself up to her full height, her eyes glowed like live coals, she took a few steps towards the door—

"I must dance—let me dance!" she gasped, and fell stiffly forward on the floor—dead.

THE FÊTE AT COQUEVILLE

BY EMILE ZOLA

THE FÊTE AT COQUEVILLE

BY EMILE ZOLA

I

COQUEVILLE is a little village planted in a cleft in the rocks, two leagues from Grandport. A fine sandy beach stretches in front of the huts lodged half-way up in the side of the cliff like shells left there by the tide. As one climbs to the heights of Grandport, on the left the yellow sheet of sand can be very clearly seen to the west like a river of gold dust streaming from the gaping cleft in the rock; and with good eyes one can even distinguish the houses, whose tones of rust spot the rock and whose chimneys send up their bluish trails to the very crest of the great slope, streaking the sky. It is a deserted hole. Coqueville has never been able to attain to the figure of two hundred inhabitants. The gorge which opens into the sea, and on the threshold of which the village is planted, burrows into the earth by turns so abrupt and by descents so steep that it is almost impossible to pass there with wagons. It cuts off all communication and isolates the country so that one seems to be a hundred leagues from the neighboring hamlets.

Translated by L. G. Meyer. Copyright, 1907, by P. F. Collier & Son.

Moreover, the inhabitants have communication with Grandport only by water. Nearly all of them fishermen, living by the ocean, they carry their fish there every day in their barks. A great commission house, the firm of Dufeu, buys their fish on contract. The father Dufeu has been dead some years, but the widow Dufeu has continued the business; she has simply engaged a clerk, M. Mouchel, a big blond devil, charged with beating up the coast and dealing with the fishermen. This M. Mouchel is the sole link between Coqueville and the civilized world.

Coqueville merits a historian. It seems certain that the village, in the night of time, was founded by the Mahés; a family which happened to establish itself there and which grew vigorous at the foot of the cliff. These Mahés continued to prosper at first, marrying continually among themselves, for during centuries one finds none but Mahés there. Then under Louis XIII appeared one Floche. No one knew too much of where he came from. He married a Mahé, and from that time a phenomenon was brought forth; the Floches in their turn prospered and multiplied exceedingly, so that they ended little by little in absorbing the Mahés, whose numbers diminished until their fortune passed entirely into the hands of the newcomers. Without doubt, the Floches brought new blood, more vigorous physical organs, a temperament which adapted itself better to that hard condition of high wind and of high

THE FÊTE AT COQUEVILLE

THE FÊTE AT COQUEVILLE

sea. At any rate, they are to-day masters of Coqueville.

It can easily be understood that this displacement of numbers and of riches was not accomplished without terrible disturbances. The Mahés and the Floches detest each other. Between them is a hatred of centuries. The Mahés in spite of their decline retain the pride of ancient conquerors. After all they are the founders, the ancestors. They speak with contempt of the first Floche, a beggar, a vagabond picked up by them from feelings of pity, and to have given away one of their daughters to whom was their eternal regret. This Floche, to hear them speak, had engendered nothing but a descent of libertines and thieves, who pass their nights in raising children and their days in coveting legacies. And there is not an insult they do not heap upon the powerful tribe of Floche, seized with that bitter rage of nobles, decimated, ruined, who see the spawn of the bourgeoisie master of their rents and of their château. The Floches, on their side, naturally have the insolence of those who triumph. They are in full possession, a thing to make them insolent. Full of contempt for the ancient race of the Mahés, they threaten to drive them from the village if they do not bow their heads. To them they are starvelings, who instead of draping themselves in their rags would do much better to mend them.

So Coqueville finds itself a prey to two fierce

109

factions—something like one hundred and thirty inhabitants bent upon devouring the other fifty for the simple reason that they are the stronger.

The struggle between two great empires has no other history.

Among the quarrels which have lately upset Coqueville, they cite the famous enmity of the brothers, Fouasse and Tupain, and the ringing battles of the Rouget ménage. You must know that every inhabitant in former days received a surname, which has become to-day the regular name of the family; for it was difficult to distinguish one's self among the cross-breedings of the Mahés and the Floches. Rouget assuredly had an ancestor of fiery blood. As for Fouasse and Tupain, they were called thus without knowing why, many surnames having lost all rational meaning in course of time. Well, old Françoise, a wanton of eighty years who lived forever, had had Fouasse by a Mahé, then becoming a widow, she remarried with a Floche and brought forth Tupain. Hence the hatred of the two brothers, made specially lively by the question of inheritance. At the Rouget's they beat each other to a jelly because Rouget accused his wife, Marie, of being unfaithful to him for a Floche, the tall Brisemotte, a strong, dark man, on whom he had already twice thrown himself with a knife, yelling that he would rip open his belly. Rouget, a small, nervous man, was a great spitfire.

But that which interested Coqueville most

deeply was neither the tantrums of Rouget nor the differences between Tupain and Fouasse. A great rumor circulated: Delphin, a Mahé, a rascal of twenty years, dared to love the beautiful Margot, the daughter of La Queue, the richest of the Floches and chief man of the country. This La Queue was, in truth, a considerable personage. They called him La Queue because his father, in the days of Louis Philippe, had been the last to tie up his hair, with the obstinacy of old age that clings to the fashions of its youth. Well, then, La Queue owned one of the two large fishing smacks of Coqueville, the "Zephir," by far the best, still quite new and seaworthy. The other big boat, the "Baleine," a rotten old patache,[1] belonged to Rouget, whose sailors were Delphin and Fouasse, while La Queue took with him Tupain and Brisemotte. These last had grown weary of laughing contemptuously at the "Baleine"; a sabot, they said, which would disappear some fine day under the billows like a handful of mud. So when La Queue learned that that ragamuffin of a Delphin, the froth of the "Baleine," allowed himself to go prowling around his daughter, he delivered two sound whacks at Margot, a trifle merely to warn her that she should never be the wife of a Mahé. As a result, Margot, furious, declared that she would pass that pair of slaps on to Delphin if he ever ventured to rub against her skirts. It was vexing

[1] Naval term signifying a rickety old concern.

to be boxed on the ears for a boy whom she had never looked in the face!

Margot, at sixteen years strong as a man and handsome as a lady, had the reputation of being a scornful person, very hard on lovers. And from that, added to the trifle of the two slaps, of the presumptuousness of Delphin, and of the wrath of Margot, one ought easily to comprehend the endless gossip of Coqueville.

Notwithstanding, certain persons said that Margot, at bottom, was not so very furious at sight of Delphin circling around her. This Delphin was a little blonde, with skin bronzed by the sea-glare, and with a mane of curly hair that fell over his eyes and in his neck. And very powerful despite his slight figure; quite capable of thrashing any one three times his size. They said that at times he ran away and passed the night in Grandport. That gave him the reputation of a werwolf with the girls, who accused him, among themselves, of "making a life of it"—a vague expression in which they included all sorts of unknown pleasures. Margot, when she spoke of Delphin, betrayed too much feeling. He, smiling with an artful air, looked at her with eyes half shut and glittering, without troubling himself the least in the world over her scorn or her transports of passion. He passed before her door, he glided along by the bushes watching for her hours at a time, full of the patience and the cunning of a cat lying in wait for a tomtit; and

112

when suddenly she discovered him behind her skirts, so close to her at times that she guessed it by the warmth of his breath, he did not fly, he took on an air gentle and melancholy which left her abashed, stifled, not regaining her wrath until he was some distance away. Surely, if her father saw her he would smite her again. But she boasted in vain that Delphin would some day get that pair of slaps she had promised him; she never seized the moment to apply them when he was there; which made people say that she ought not to talk so much, since in the end she kept the slaps herself.

No one, however, supposed she could ever be Delphin's wife. In her case they saw the weakness of a coquette. As for a marriage between the most beggarly of the Mahés, a fellow who had not six shirts to set up housekeeping with, and the daughter of the mayor, the richest heiress of the Floches, it would seem simply monstrous.

Evil tongues insinuated that she could perfectly go with him all the same, but that she would certainly not marry him. A rich girl takes her pleasure as it suits her; only, if she has a head, she does not commit a folly. Finally all Coqueville interested itself in the matter, curious to know how things would turn out. Would Delphin get his two slaps? or else Margot, would she let herself be kissed on both cheeks in some hole in the cliff? They must see! There were some for the slaps and there were some for the kisses. Coqueville was in revolution.

In the village two people only, the curé and the *garde champêtre*,[2] belonged neither to the Mahés nor to the Floches. The *garde champêtre*, a tall, dried-up fellow, whose name no one knew, but who was called the Emperor, no doubt because he had served under Charles X, as a matter of fact exercised no burdensome supervison over the commune which was all bare rocks and waste lands. A sub-prefect who patronized him had created for him the sinecure where he devoured in peace his very small living.

As for the Abbé Radiguet, he was one of those simple-minded priests whom the bishop, in his desire to be rid of him, buries in some out of the way hole. He lived the life of an honest man, once more turned peasant, hoeing his little garden redeemed from the rock, smoking his pipe and watching his salads grow. His sole fault was a gluttony which he knew not how to refine, reduced to adoring mackerel and to drinking, at times, more cider than he could contain. In other respects, the father of his parishioners, who came at long intervals to hear a mass to please him.

But the curé and the *garde champêtre* were obliged to take sides after having succeeded for a long time in remaining neutral. Now, the Emperor held for the Mahés, while the Abbé Radi-

2 Watchman.

guet supported the Floches. Hence complications. As the Emperor, from morning to night, lived like a bourgeois [citizen], and as he wearied of counting the boats which put out from Grandport, he took it upon himself to act as village police. Having become the partizan of the Mahés, through native instinct for the preservation of society, he sided with Fouasse against Tupain; he tried to catch the wife of Rouget in *flagrante delicto* with Brisemotte, and above all he closed his eyes when he saw Delphin slipping into Margot's courtyard. The worst of it was that these tactics brought about heated quarrels between the Emperor and his natural superior, the mayor La Queue. Respectful of discipline, the former heard the reproaches of the latter, then recommenced to act as his head dictated; which disorganized the public authority of Coqueville. One could not pass before the shed ornamented with the name of the town hall without being deafened by the noise of some dispute. On the other hand, the Abbé Radiguet rallied to the triumphant Floches, who loaded him with superb mackerel, secretly encouraged the resistance of Rouget's wife and threatened Margot with the flames of hell if she should ever allow Delphin to touch her with his finger. It was, to sum up, complete anarchy; the army in revolt against the civil power, religion making itself complaisant toward the pleasures of the bourgeoisie; a whole people, a hundred and eighty inhabitants, devouring each other in a hole, in face of the vast sea, and of the infinite sky.

Alone, in the midst of topsy-turvy Coqueville, Delphin preserved the laughter of a love-sick boy, who scorned the rest, provided Margot was for him. He followed her zigzags as one follows hares. Very wise, despite his simple look, he wanted the curé to marry them, so that his bliss might last forever.

One evening, in a byway where he was watching for her, Margot at last raised her hand. But she stopped, all red; for without waiting for the slap, he had seized the hand that threatened him and kissed it furiously. As she trembled, he said to her in a low voice: "I love you. Won't you have me?"

"Never!" she cried, in rebellion.

He shrugged his shoulders, then with an air, calm and tender, "Pray do not say that—we shall be very comfortable together, we two. You will see how nice it is."

II

That Sunday the weather was appalling, one of those sudden calamities of September that unchain such fearful tempests on the rocky coast of Grandport. At nightfall Coqueville sighted a ship in distress driven by the wind. But the shadows deepened, they could not dream of rendering help. Since the evening before, the

THE FETE AT COQUEVILLE

"Zéphir" and the "Baleine" had been moored in the little natural harbor situated at the left of the beach, between two walls of granite. Neither La Queue nor Rouget had dared to go out, the worst of it was that M. Mouchel, representing the Widow Dufeu, had taken the trouble to come in person that Saturday to promise them a reward if they would make a serious effort; fish was scarce, they were complaining at the markets. So, Sunday evening, going to bed under squalls of rain, Coqueville growled in a bad humor. It was the everlasting story: orders kept coming in while the sea guarded its fish. And all the village talked of the ship which they had seen passing in the hurricane, and which must assuredly by that time be sleeping at the bottom of the water. The next day, Monday, the sky was dark as ever. The sea, still high, raged without being able to calm itself, although the wind was blowing less strong. It fell completely, but the waves kept up their furious motion. In spite of everything, the two boats went out in the afternoon. Toward four o'clock, the "Zéphir" came in again, having caught nothing. While the sailors, Tupain and Brisemotte, anchored in the little harbor, La Queue, exasperated, on the shore, shook his fist at the ocean. And M. Mouchel was waiting! Margot was there, with the half of Coqueville, watching the last surgings of the tempest, sharing her father's rancor against the sea and the sky.

"But where is the 'Baleine'?" demanded some one.

"Out there beyond the point," said La Queue. "If that carcass comes back whole to-day, it will be by a chance."

He was full of contempt. Then he informed them that it was good for the Mahés to risk their skins in that way; when one is not worth a sou, one may perish. As for him, he preferred to break his word to M. Mouchel.

In the meantime, Margot was examining the point of rocks behind which the "Baleine" was hidden.

"Father," she asked at last, "have they caught something?"

"They?" he cried. "Nothing at all."

He calmed himself and added more gently, seeing the Emperor, who was sneering at him:

"I do not know whether they have caught anything, but as they never do catch anything—"

"Perhaps, to-day, all the same, they have taken something," said the Emperor ill-naturedly. "Such things have been seen." La Queue was about to reply angrily. But the Abbé Radiguet, who came up, calmed him. From the porch of the church the abbé had happened to observe the "Baleine"; and the bark seemed to be giving chase to some big fish. This news greatly interested Coqueville. In the groups reunited on the shore there were Mahés and Floches, the former praying that the boat might come in with a miraculous catch, the others making vows that it might come in empty.

Margot, holding herself very straight, did not take her eyes from the sea. "There they are!" said she simply.

And in fact a black dot showed itself beyond the point. All looked at it. One would have said a cork dancing on the water. The Emperor did not see even the black dot. One must be of Coqueville to recognize at that distance the "Baleine" and those who manned her.

"See!" said Margot, who had the best eyes of the coast, "it is Fouasse and Rouget who are rowing— The little one is standing up in the bow."

She called Delphin "the little one" so as not to mention his name. And from then on they followed the course of the bark, trying to account for her strange movements. As the curé said, she appeared to be giving chase to some great fish that might be fleeing before her. That seemed extraordinary. The Emperor pretended that their net was without doubt being carried away. But La Queue cried that they were do-nothings, and that they were just amusing themselves. Quite certain they were not fishing for seals! All the Floches made merry over that joke; while the Mahés, vexed, declared that Rouget was a fine fellow all the same, and that he was risking his skin while others at the least puff of wind preferred *terra firma*. The Abbé Radiguet was forced to interpose again for there were slaps in the air.

"What ails them?" said Margot abruptly. "They are off again!" They ceased menacing one another, and every eye searched the horizon. The "Baleine" was once more hidden behind the point. This time La Queue himself became uneasy. He could not account for such maneuvres. The fear that Rouget was really in a fair way to catch some fish threw him off his mental balance. No one left the beach, although there was nothing strange to be seen. They stayed there nearly two hours, they watched incessantly for the bark, which appeared from time to time, then disappeared. It finished by not showing itself at all any more. La Queue, enraged, breathing in his heart the abominable wish, declared that she must have sunk; and, as just at that moment Rouget's wife appeared with Brisemotte, he looked at them both, sneering, while he patted Tupain on the shoulder to console him already for the death of his brother, Fouasse. But he stopped laughing when he caught sight of his daughter Margot, silent and looming, her eyes on the distance; it was quite possibly for Delphin.

"What are you up to over there?" he scolded. "Be off home with you! Mind, Margot!"

She did not stir. Then all at once: "Ah! there they are!"

He gave a cry of surprise. Margot, with her

good eyes, swore that she no longer saw a soul in the bark; neither Rouget, nor Fouasse, nor any one! The "Baleine," as if abandoned, ran before the wind, tacking about every minute, rocking herself with a lazy air.

A west wind had fortunately risen and was driving her toward the land, but with strange caprices which tossed her to right and to left. Then all Coqueville ran down to the shore. One half shouted to the other half, there remained not a girl in the houses to look after the soup. It was a catastrophe; something inexplicable, the strangeness of which completely turned their heads. Marie, the wife of Rouget, after a moment's reflection, thought it her duty to burst into tears. Tupain succeeded in merely carrying an air of affliction. All the Mahés were in great distress, while the Floches tried to appear conventional. Margot collapsed as if she had her legs broken.

"What are you up to again!" cried La Queue, who stumbled upon her.

"I am tired," she answered simply.

And she turned her face toward the sea, her cheeks between her hands, shading her eyes with the ends of her fingers, gazing fixedly at the bark rocking itself idly on the waves with the air of a good fellow who has drunk too much.

In the meanwhile suppositions were rife. Perhaps the three men had fallen into the water? Only, all three at a time, that seemed absurd.

La Queue would have liked well to persuade them that the "Baleine" had gone to pieces like a rotten egg; but the boat still held the sea; they shrugged their shoulders. Then, as if the three men had actually perished, he remembered that he was Mayor and spoke of formalities.

"Leave off!" cried the Emperor, "Does one die in such a silly way?" "If they had fallen overboard, little Delphin would have been here by this!"

All Coqueville had to agree, Delphin swam like a herring. But where then could the three men be? They shouted: "I tell you, yes!"—"I tell you, no!"—"Too stupid!"—"Stupid yourself!" And matters came to the point of exchanging blows. The Abbé Radiguet was obliged to make an appeal for reconciliation, while the Emperor hustled the crowd about to establish order. Meanwhile, the bark, without haste, continued to dance before the world. It waltzed, seeming to mock at the people; the sea carried her in, making her salute the land in long rhythmic reverences. Surely it was a bark in a crazy fit. Margot, her cheeks between her hands, kept always gazing. A yawl had just put out of the harbor to go to meet the "Baleine." It was Brisemotte, who had exhibited that impatience, as if he had been delayed in giving certainty to Rouget's wife. From that moment all Coqueville interested itself in the yawl. The voices rose higher: "Well, does he see anything?"

The "Baleine" advanced with her mysterious
and mocking air. At last they saw him draw
himself up and look into the bark that he had
succeeded in taking in tow. All held their
breath. But, abruptly, he burst out laughing.
That was a surprise; what had he to be amused
at? "What is it? What have you got there?"
they shouted to him furiously.

He, without replying, laughed still louder.
He made gestures as if to say that they would
see. Then having fastened the "Baleine" to the
yawl, he towed her back. And an unlooked-for
spectacle stunned Coqueville. In the bottom of
the bark, the three men—Rouget, Delphin,
Fouasse—were beatifically stretched out on their
backs, snoring, with fists clenched, dead drunk. In
their midst was found a little cask stove in, some
full cask they had come across at sea and which
they had appreciated. Without doubt, it was
very good, for they had drunk it all save a liter's
worth which had leaked into the bark and which
was mixed with the sea water.

"Ah! the pig!" cried the wife of Rouget,
brutally, ceasing to whimper.

"Well, it's characteristic—their catch!" said
La Queue, who affected great disgust.

"Forsooth!" replied the Emperor, "they catch
what they can! They have at least caught a
cask, while others have not caught anything
at all."

The Mayor shut up, greatly vexed. Coqueville brayed. They understood now. When barks are intoxicated, they dance as men do; and that one, in truth, had her belly full of liquor. Ah, the slut! What a minx! She festooned over the ocean with the air of a sot who could no longer recognize his home. And Coqueville laughed, and fumed, the Mahés found it funny, while the Floches found it disgusting. They surrounded the "Baleine," they craned their necks, they strained their eyes to see sleeping there the three jolly dogs who were exposing the secret springs of their jubilation, oblivious of the crowd hanging over them. The abuse and the laughter troubled them but little. Rouget did not hear his wife accuse him of drinking up all they had; Fouasse did not feel the stealthy kicks with which his brother Tupain rammed his sides. As for Delphin, he was pretty, after he had drunk, with his blond hair, his rosy face drowned in bliss. Margot had gotten up, and silently, for the present, she contemplated the little fellow with a hard expression.

"Must put them to bed!" cried a voice.

But just then Delphin opened his eyes. He rolled looks of rapture over the people. They questioned him on all sides with an eagerness that dazed him somewhat, the more easily since he was still as drunk as a thrush.

"Well! What?" he stuttered; "it was a little cask— There is no fish. Therefore, we have caught a little cask."

THE FÊTE AT COQUEVILLE

He did not get beyond that. To every sentence he added simply: "It was very good!"

"But what was it in the cask?" they asked him hotly.

"Ah! I don't know—it was very good."

By this time Coqueville was burning to know. Every one lowered their noses to the boat, sniffing vigorously. With one opinion, it smelt of liquor; only no one could guess what liquor. The Emperor, who flattered himself that he had drunk of everything that a man can drink, said that he would see. He solemnly took in the palm of his hand a little of the liquor that was swimming in the bottom of the bark. The crowd became all at once silent. They waited. But the Emperor, after sucking up a mouthful, shook his head as if still badly informed. He sucked twice, more and more embarrassed, with an air of uneasiness and surprise. And he was bound to confess:

"I do not know— It's strange— If there was no salt water in it, I would know, no doubt— My word of honor, it is very strange!"

They looked at him. They stood struck with awe before that which the Emperor himself did not venture to pronounce. Coqueville contemplated with respect the little empty cask.

"It was very good!" once more said Delphin, who seemed to be making game of the people. Then, indicating the sea with a comprehensive sweep, he added: "If you want some, there is

125

more there—I saw them—little casks—little casks—little casks—"

And he rocked himself with the refrain which he kept singing, gazing tenderly at Margot. He had just caught sight of her. Furious, she made a motion as if to slap him; but he did not even close his eyes; he awaited the slap with an air of tenderness.

The Abbé Radiguet, puzzled by that unknown tipple, he, too, dipped his finger in the bark and sucked it. Like the Emperor, he shook his head: no, he was not familiar with that, it was very extraordinary. They agreed on but one point: the cask must have been wreckage from the ship in distress, signaled Sunday evening. The English ships often carried to Grandport such cargoes of liquor and fine wines.

Little by little the day faded and the people were withdrawn into shadow. But La Queue remained absorbed, tormented by an idea which he no longer expressed. He stopped, he listened a last time to Delphin, whom they were carrying along, and who was repeating in his sing-song voice: "Little casks—little casks—little casks—if you want some, there are more!"

III

That night the weather changed completely. When Coqueville awoke the following day an unclouded sun was shining; the sea spread out

without a wrinkle, like a great piece of green
satin. And it was warm, one of those pale glows
of autumn.

First of the village, La Queue had risen, still
clouded from the dreams of the night. He kept
looking for a long time toward the sea, to the
right, to the left. At last, with a sour look, he
said that he must in any event satisfy M.
Mouchel. And he went away at once with Tupain
and Brisemotte, threatening Margot to touch up
her sides if she did not walk straight. As the
"Zéphir" left the harbor, and as he saw the
"Baleine" swinging heavily at her anchor, he
cheered up a little saying: "To-day, I guess, not
a bit of it! Blow out the candle, Jeanetton! those
gentlemen have gone to bed!"

And as soon as the "Zéphir" had reached the
open sea, La Queue cast his nets. After that he
went to visit his "jambins." The jambins are a
kind of elongated eel-pot in which they catch
more, especially lobsters and red gurnet. But in
spite of the calm sea, he did well to visit his jambins one by one. All were empty; at the bottom
of the last one, as if in mockery, he found a little
mackerel, which he threw back angrily into the
sea. It was fate; there were weeks like that when
the fish flouted Coqueville, and always at a time
when M. Mouchel had expressed a particular desire for them. When La Queue drew in his nets,
an hour later, he found nothing but a bunch of
seaweed. Straightway he swore, his fists

clenched, raging so much the more for the vast
serenity of the ocean, lazy and sleeping like a
sheet of burnished silver under the blue sky.
The "Zéphir," without a waver, glided along in
gentle ease. La Queue decided to go in again,
after having cast his nets once more. In the
afternoon he came to see them, and he menaced
God and the saints, cursing in abominable words.

In the meanwhile, Rouget, Fouasse, and Delphin kept on sleeping. They did not succeed in
standing up until the dinner hour. They recol-
lected nothing, they were conscious only of having been treated to something extraordinary,
something which they did not understand. In
the afternoon, as they were all three down at the
harbor, the Emperor tried to question them concerning the liquor, now that they had recovered
their senses. It was like, perhaps, eau-de-vie
with liquorice-juice in it; or rather one might
say rum, sugared and burned. They said "Yes";
they said "No." From their replies, the Emperor suspected that it was ratafia; but he would
not have sworn to it. That day Rouget and his
men had too many pains in their sides to go
a-fishing. Moreover, they knew that La Queue
had gone out without success that morning, and
they talked of waiting until the next day before
visiting their jambins. All three of them, seated
on blocks of stone, watched the tide come in, their
backs rounded, their mouths clammy, half-
asleep.

But suddenly Delphin woke up; he jumped on to the stone, his eyes on the distance, crying: "Look, Boss, off there!"

"What?" asked Rouget, who stretched his limbs.

"A cask."

Rouget and Fouasse were at once on their feet, their eyes gleaming, sweeping the horizon.

"Where is it, lad? Where is the cask?" repeated the boss, greatly moved.

"Off there—to the left—that black spot."

The others saw nothing. Then Rouget swore an oath. "Nom de Dieu!"

He had just spotted the cask, big as a lentil on the white water in a slanting ray of the setting sun. And he ran to the "Baleine," followed by Delphin and Fouasse, who darted forward tapping their backs with their heels and making the pebbles roll.

The "Baleine" was just putting out from the harbor when the news that they saw a cask out at sea was circulated in Coqueville. The children, the women, began to run. They shouted: "A cask! a cask!"

"Do you see it? The current is driving it toward Grandport."

"Ah, yes! on the left—a cask! Come, quick!"

And Coqueville came; tumbled down from its rock; the children arrived head over heels, while the women picked up their skirts with both hands to descend quickly. Soon the entire village was on the beach as on the night before.

Marget showed herself for an instant, then she ran back at full speed to the house, where she wished to forestall her father, who was discussing an official process with the Emperor. At last La Queue appeared. He was livid; he said to the *garde champêtre:* "Hold your peace! It's Rouget who has sent you here to beguile me. Well, then, he shall not get it. You'll see!"

When he saw the "Baleine," three hundred metres out, making with all her oars toward the black dot, rocking in the distance, his fury redoubled. And he shoved Tupain and Brisemotte into the "Zéphir," and he pulled out in turn, repeating: "No, they shall not have it; I'll die sooner!"

Then Coqueville had a fine spectacle; a mad race between the "Zéphir" and the "Baleine." When the latter saw the first leave the harbor, she understood the danger, and shot off with all her speed. She may have been four hundred metres ahead; but the chances remained even, for the "Zéphir" was otherwise light and swift; so excitement was at its height on the beach. The Mahès and the Floches had instinctively formed into two groups, following eagerly the vicissitudes of the struggle, each upholding its own boat. At first the "Baleine" kept her advantage, but as soon as the "Zéphir" spread herself, they saw that she was gaining little by little. The

"Baleine" made a supreme effort and succeeded for a few minutes in holding her distance. Then the "Zéphir" once more gained upon the "Baleine," came up with her at extraordinary speed. From that moment on, it was evident that the two barks would meet in the neighborhood of the cask. Victory hung on a circumstance, on the slightest mishap.

"The 'Baleine'! The 'Baleine'!" cried the Mahés.

But they soon ceased shouting. When the "Baleine" was almost touching the cask, the "Zephir," by a bold maneuvre, managed to pass in front of her and throw the cask to the left, where La Queue harpooned it with a thrust of the boat-hook.

"The 'Zéphir'! the 'Zéphir'!" screamed the Floches.

And the Emperor, having spoken of foul play, big words were exchanged. Margot clapped her hands. The Abbé Radiguet came down with his breviary, made a profound remark which abruptly calmed the people, and then threw them into consternation.

"They will, perhaps, drink it all, these, too," he murmured with a melancholy air.

At sea, between the "Baleine" and the "Zéphir," a violent quarrel broke out. Rouget called La Queue a thief, while the latter called Rouget a good-for-nothing. The men even took up their oars to beat each other down, and the adventure lacked little of turning into a naval combat. More than this, they engaged to meet on land, showing their fists and theatening to disembowel each other as soon as they found each other again.

"The rascal!" grumbled Rouget. "You know, that cask is bigger than the one of yesterday. It's yellow, this one—it ought to be great." Then in accents of despair: "Let's go and see the jambins; there may very possibly be lobsters in them."

And the "Baleine" went on heavily to the left, steering toward the point.

In the "Zéphir," La Queue had to get in a passion in order to hold Tupain and Brisemotte from the cask. The boat-hook, in smashing a hoop, had made a leaking for the red liquid, which the two men tasted from the ends of their fingers and which they found exquisite. One might easily drink a glass without its producing much effect. But La Queue would not have it. He caulked the cask and declared that the first who sucked it should have a talk with him. On land, they would see.

"Then," asked Tupain, sullenly, "are we going to draw out the jambins?"

"Yes, right away; there is no hurry!" replied La Queue.

He also gazed lovingly at the barrel. He felt his limbs melt with longing to go in at once and taste it. The fish bored him.

THE FÊTE AT COQUEVILLE

"Bah!" said he at the end of a silence. "Let's go back, for it's late. We will return to-morrow." And he was relaxing his fishing when he noticed another cask at his right, this one very small, and which stood on end, turning on itself like a top. That was the last straw for the nets and the jambins. No one even spoke of them any longer. The "Zéphir" gave chase to the little barrel, which was caught very easily.

During this time a similar adventure overtook the "Baleine." After Rouget had already visited five jambins completely empty, Delphin, always on the watch, cried out that he saw something. But it did not have the appearance of a cask, it was too long.

"It's a beam," said Fouasse.

Rouget let fall his sixth jambin without drawing it out of the water. "Let's go and see, all the same," said he.

As they advanced, they thought they recognized at first a beam, a chest, the trunk of a tree. Then they gave a cry of joy.

It was a real cask, but a very queer cask, such as they had never seen before. One would have said a tube, bulging in the middle and closed at the two ends by a layer of plaster.

"Ah, that's comical!" cried Rouget, in rapture. "This one I want the Emperor to taste. Come, children, let's go in."

They all agreed not to touch it, and the "Baleine" returned to Coqueville at the same

133

moment as the "Zéphir," in its turn, anchored in the little harbor. Not one inquisitive had left the beach. Cries of joy greeted that unexpected catch of three casks. The *gamins* hurled their caps into the air, while the women had at once gone on the run to look for glasses. It was decided to taste the liquid on the spot. The wreckage belonged to the village. Not one protest arose. Only they formed into two groups, the Mahés surrounded Rouget, the Floches would not let go of La Queue.

"Emperor, the first glass for you!" cried Rouget. "Tell us what it is."

The liquor was of a beautiful golden yellow. The *garde champêtre* raised his glass, looked at it, smelt it, then decided to drink.

"That comes from Holland," said he, after a long silence.

He did not give any other information. All the Mahés drank with deference. It was rather thick, and they stood surprised, for it tasted of flowers. The women found it very good. As for the men, they would have preferred less sugar. Nevertheless, at the bottom it ended by being strong at the third or fourth glass. The more they drank, the better they liked it. The men became jolly, the women grew funny.

But the Emperor, in spite of his recent quarrels with the Mayor, had gone to hang about the group of Floches.

The biggest cask gave out a dark-red liquor, while they drew from the smallest a liquid white as water from the rock; and it was this latter that was the stiffest, a regular pepper, something that skinned the tongue.

Not one of the Floches recognized it, neither the red nor the white.

There were, however, some wags there. It annoyed them to be regaling themselves without knowing over what.

"I say, Emperor, taste that for me!" said La Queue, thus taking the first step.

The Emperor, who had been waiting for the invitation, posed once more as connoisseur.

"As for the red," he said, "there is orange in that! And for the white," he declared, "that— that is excellent!"

They had to content themselves with these replies, for he shook his head with a knowing air, with the happy look of a man who has given satisfaction to the world.

The Abbé Radiguet, alone, did not seem convinced. As for him, he had the names on the tip of his tongue; and to thoroughly reassure himself, he drank small glasses, one after the other, repeating: "Wait, wait, I know what it is. In a moment I will tell you."

In the mean while, little by little, merriment grew in the group of the Mahés and the group of the Floches. The latter, particularly, laughed very loud because they had mixed the liquors, a thing that excited them the more. For the rest, the one and the other of the groups kept apart. They did not offer each other of their casks, they simply cast sympathetic glances, seized with the unavowed desire to taste their neighbor's liquor, which might possibly be better. The inimical brothers, Tupain and Fouasse, were in close proximity all the evening without showing their fists. It was remarked, also, that Rouget and his wife drank from the same glass. As for Margot, she distributed the liquor among the Floches, and as she filled the glasses too full, and the liquor ran over her fingers, she kept sucking them continually, so well that, though obeying her father who forbade her to drink, she became as fuddled as a girl in vintage time. It was not unbecoming to her; on the contrary, she got rosy all over, her eyes were like candles.

The sun set, the evening was like the softness of springtime. Coqueville had finished the casks and did not dream of going home to dine. They found themselves too comfortable on the beach. When it was pitch night, Margot, sitting apart, felt some one blowing on her neck. It was Delphin, very gay, walking on all fours, prowling behind her like a wolf. She repressed a cry so as not to awaken her father, who would have sent Delphin a kick in the back.

"Go away, imbecile!" she murmured, half angry, half laughing; "you will get yourself caught!"

THE FÊTE AT COQUEVILLE

IV

The following day Coqueville, in rising, found the sun already high above the horizon. The air was softer still, a drowsy sea under a clear sky, one of those times of laziness when it is so good to do nothing. It was a Wednesday. Until breakfast time, Coqueville rested from the fête of the previous evening. Then they went down to the beach to see.

That Wednesday the fish, the Widow Dufeu, M. Mouchel, all were forgotten. La Queue and Rouget did not even speak of visiting their jambins. Toward three o'clock they sighted some casks. Four of them were dancing before the village. The "Zéphir" and the "Baleine" went in chase; but as there was enough for all, they disputed no longer. Each boat had its share. At six o'clock, after having swept all over the little gulf, Rouget and La Queue came in, each with three casks. And the fête began again. The women had brought down tables for convenience. They had brought benches as well; they set up two cafés in the open air, such as they had at Grandport. The Mahés were on the left; the Floches on the right, still separated by a bar of sand. Nevertheless, that evening the Emperor, who went from one group to the other, carried his glasses full, so at to give every one a taste of the six casks. At about nine o'clock they were much gayer than the night before.

137

The next day Coqueville could never remember how it had gone to bed.

Thursday the "Zéphir" and the "Baleine" caught but four casks, two each, but they were enormous. Friday the fishing was superb, undreamed of; there were seven casks, three for Rouget and four for La Queue. Coqueville was entering upon a golden age. They never did anything any more. The fishermen, working off the alcohol of the night before, slept till noon. Then they strolled down to the beach and interrogated the sea. Their sole anxiety was to know what liquor the sea was going to bring them. They waited there for hours, their eyes strained; they raised shouts of joy when wreckage appeared.

The women and the children, from the tops of the rocks, pointed with sweeping gestures even to the least bunch of seaweed rolled in by the waves. And, at all hours, the "Zéphir" and the "Baleine" stood ready to leave. They put out, they beat the gulf, they fished for casks, as they had fished for tun; disdaining now the tame mackerel who capered about in the sun, and the lazy sole rocked on the foam of the water. Coqueville watched the fishing, dying of laughter on the sands. Then in the evening they drank the catch.

That which enraptured Coqueville was that the casks did not cease. When there were no more, there were still more! The ship that had been lost must truly have had a pretty cargo aboard;

and Coqueville became egoist and merry, joked over the wrecked ship, a regular wine-cellar, enough to intoxicate all the fish of the ocean. Added to that, never did they catch two casks alike; they were of all shapes, of all sizes, of all colors. Then, in every cask there was a different liquor. So the Emperor was plunged into profound reveries; he who had drunk everything, he could identify nothing any more. La Queue declared that never had he seen such a cargo. The Abbé Radiguet guessed it was an order from some savage king, wishing to set up his wine-cellar. Coqueville, rocked in mysterious intoxication, no longer tried to understand.

The ladies preferred the "creams"; they had cream of mocha, of cacao, of mint, of vanilla. Marie Rouget drank one night so much anisette that she was sick.

Margot and the other young ladies tapped the curaçao, the benedictine, the trappistine, the chartreuse. As to the cassis, it was reserved for the little children. Naturally the men rejoiced more when they caught cognacs, rums, gins, everything that burned the mouth. Then surprises produced themselves. A cask of *raki* of Chio, flavored with mastic, stupefied Coqueville, which thought that it had fallen on a cask of essence of turpentine. All the same they drank it, for they must lose nothing; but they talked about it for a long time. Arrack from Batavia, Swedish eau-de-vie with cumin, tuica calugaresca from Rumania, slivowitz from Servia, all equally overturned every idea that Coqueville had of what one should endure. At heart they had a weakness for kümmel and kirschwasser, for liqueurs as pale as water and stiff enough to kill a man.

Heavens! was it possible so many good things had been invented! At Coqueville they had known nothing but eau-de-vie; and, moreover, not every one at that. So their imaginations finished in exultation; they arrived at a state of veritable worship, in face of that inexhaustible variety, for that which intoxicates. Oh! to get drunk every night on something new, on something one does not even know the name of! It seemed like a fairy-tale, a rain, a fountain, that would spout extraordinary liquids, all the distilled alcohols, perfumed with all the flowers and all the fruits of creation.

So then, Friday evening, there were seven casks on the beach! Coqueville did not leave the beach. They lived there, thanks to the mildness of the season. Never in September had they enjoyed so fine a week. The fête had lasted since Monday, and there was no reason why it should not last forever if Providence should continue to send them casks; for the Abbé Radiguet saw therein the hand of Providence. All business was suspended; what use drudging when pleasure came to them in their sleep? They were all bourgeois, bourgeois who were drinking expensive liquors without having to pay anything at the café. With hands in pocket, Coqueville basked in the sunshine waiting for the evening's spree. Moreover, it did not sober up; it enjoyed side by side the gaieties of kümmel, of kirsch-wasser, of ratafia; in seven days they knew the wraths of gin, the tendernesses of curaçao, the laughter of cognac. And Coqueville remained as innocent as a new-born child, knowing nothing about anything, drinking with conviction that which the good Lord sent them.

It was on Friday that the Mahés and the Floches fraternized. They were very jolly that evening. Already, the evening before, distances had drawn nearer, the most intoxicated had trodden down the bar of sand which separated the two groups. There remained but one step to take. On the side of the Floches the four casks were emptying, while the Mahés were equally finishing their three little barrels; just three liqueurs which made the French flag; one blue, one white, and one red. The blue filled the Floches with jealousy, because a blue liqueur seemed to them something really supernatural. La Queue, grown good-natured since he had been drunk, advanced, a glass in his hand, feeling that he ought to take the first step as magistrate.

"See here, Rouget," he stuttered, "will you drink with me?"

"Willingly," replied Rouget, who was stag-gering under a feeling of tenderness.

And they fell upon each other's necks. Then they all wept, so great was their emotion. The Mahés and the Floches embraced, they who had been devouring one another for three centuries. The Abbé Radiguet, greatly touched, again spoke of the finger of God. They drank to each other in the three liqueurs, the blue, the white, and the red.

"Vive la France!" cried the Emperor.

The blue was worthless, the white of not much account, but the red was really a success. Then they tapped the casks of the Floches. Then they danced. As there was no band, some good-natured boys clapped their hands, whistling, which excited the girls. The fête became superb. The seven casks were placed in a row; each could choose that which he liked best. Those who had had enough stretched themselves out on the sands, where they slept for a while; and when they awoke they began again. Little by little the others spread the fun until they took up the whole beach. Right up to midnight they skipped in the open air. The sea had a soft sound, the stars shone in a deep sky, a sky of vast peace. It was the serenity of the infant ages enveloping the joy of a tribe of savages, intoxicated by their first cask of eau-de-vie.

Nevertheless, Coqueville went home to bed again. When there was nothing more left to drink, the Floches and the Mahés helped one another, carried one another, and ended by find·

ing their beds again one way or another. On Saturday the fête lasted until nearly two o'clock in the morning. They had caught six casks, two of them enormous. Fouasse and Tupain almost fought. Tupain, who was wicked when drunk, talked of finishing his brother. But that quarrel disgusted every one, the Floches as well as the Mahés. Was it reasonable to keep on quarreling when the whole village was embracing? They forced the two brothers to drink together. They were sulky. The Emperor promised to watch them. Neither did the Rouget household get on well. When Marie had taken anisette she was prodigal in her attentions to Brisemotte, which Rouget could not behold with a calm eye, especially since having become sensitive, he also wished to be loved. The Abbé Radiguet, full of forbearance, did well in preaching forgiveness; they feared an accident.

"Bah!" said La Queue; "all will arrange itself. If the fishing is good to-morrow, you will see— Your health!"

However, La Queue himself was not yet perfect. He still kept his eye on Delphin and leveled kicks at him whenever he saw him approach Margot. The Emperor was indignant, for there was no common sense in preventing two young people from laughing. But La Queue always swore to kill his daughter sooner than give her to "the little one." Moreover, Margot would not be willing.

"Isn't it so? You are too proud," he cried. "Never would you marry a ragamuffin!"

"Never, papa!" answered Margot.

Saturday, Margot drank a great deal of sugary liqueur. No one had any idea of such sugar. As she was no longer on her guard, she soon found herself sitting close to the cask. She laughed, happy, in paradise; she saw stars, and it seemed to her that there was music within her, playing dance tunes. Then it was that Delphin slipped into the shadow of the casks. He took her hand; he asked: "Say, Margot, will you?"

She kept on smiling. Then she replied: "It is papa who will not."

"Oh! that's nothing," said the little one; "you know the old ones never will—provided you are willing, you." And he grew bold, he planted a kiss on her neck. She bridled; shivers ran along her shoulders. "Stop! You tickle me."

But she talked no more of giving him a slap. In the first place, she was not able to, for her hands were too weak. Then it seemed nice to her, those little kisses on the neck. It was like the liqueur that enervated her so deliciously. She ended by turning her head and extending her chin, just like a cat.

"There!" she stammered, "there under the ear —that tickles me. Oh! that is nice!"

They had both forgotten La Queue. Fortunately the Emperor was on guard. He pointed them out to the Abbé.

"Look there, Curé—it would be better to marry them."

"Morals would gain thereby," declared the priest sententiously.

And he charged himself with the matter for the morrow. 'Twas he himself that would speak to La Queue. Meanwhile La Queue had drunk so much that the Emperor and the Curé were forced to carry him home. On the way they tried to reason with him on the subject of his daughter; but they could draw from him nothing but growls. Behind them, in the untroubled night, Delphin led Margot home.

The next day by four o'clock the "Zéphir" and the "Baleine" had already caught seven casks. At six o'clock the "Zéphir" caught two more. That made nine.

Then Coqueville fêted Sunday. It was the seventh day that it had been drunk. And the fête was complete—a fête such as no one had ever seen, and which no one will ever see again. Speak of it in Lower Normandy, and they will tell you with laughter, "Ah! yes, the fête at Coqueville!"

V

In the mean while, since the Tuesday, M. Mouchel had been surprised at not seeing either Rouget or La Queue arrive at Grandport. What the devil could those fellows be doing? The sea was fine, the fishing ought to be splendid. Very possibly they wished to bring a whole load of soles and lobsters in all at once. And he was patient until the Wednesday.

Wednesday, M. Mouchel was angry. You must know that the Widow Dufeu was not a good-natured person. She was a woman who in a flash came to high words. Although he was a handsome fellow, blond and powerful, he trem-bled before her, especially since he had dreams of marrying her, always with little attentions, free to subdue her with a slap if he ever became her master. Well, that Wednesday morning the Widow Dufeu stormed, complaining that the bundles were no longer forwarded, that the sea failed; and she accused him of running after the girls of the coast instead of busying himself with the whiting and the mackerel which ought to be yielding in abundance. M. Mouchel, vexed, fell back on Coqueville's singular breach of honor. For a moment surprise calmed the Widow Dufeu. What was Coqueville dreaming about? Never had it so conducted itself before. But she declared immediately that she had nothing to do with Coqueville; that it was M. Mouchel's busi-ness to look into matters, that she should take a partner if he allowed himself to be played with again by the fishermen. In a word, much dis-quieted, he sent Rouget and La Queue to the devil. Perhaps, after all, they would come to-morrow.

The next day, Thursday, neither the one nor

the other appeared. Toward evening, M. Mouchel, desperate, climbed the rock to the left of Grandport, from which one could see in the distance Coqueville, with its yellow spot of beach. He gazed at it a long time. The village had a tranquil look in the sun, light smoke was rising from the chimneys; no doubt the women were preparing the soup. M. Mouchel was satisfied that Coqueville was still in its place, that a rock from the cliff had not crushed it, and he understood less and less. As he was about to descend again, he thought he could make out two black points on the gulf; the "Baleine" and the "Zéphir." After that he went back to calm the Widow Dufeu. Coqueville was fishing. The night passed. Friday was here. Still nothing of Coqueville. M. Mouchel climbed to his rock more than ten times. He was beginning to lose his head; the Widow Dufeu behaved abominably to him, without his finding anything to reply. Coqueville was always there, in the sun, warming itself like a lazy lizard. Only, M. Mouchel saw no more smoke. The village seemed dead. Had they all died in their holes? On the beach, there was quite a movement, but that might be seaweed rocked by the tide. Saturday, still no one. The Widow Dufeu scolded no more; her eyes were fixed, her lips white. M. Mouchel passed two hours on the rock. A curiosity grew in him, a purely personal need of accounting to himself for the strange immobility of the village. The old walls sleeping beatifically in the sun ended by worrying him. His resolution was taken; he would set out that Monday very early in the morning and try to get down there near nine o'clock.

It was not a promenade to go to Coqueville. M. Mouchel preferred to follow the route by land, in that way he would come upon the village without their expecting him. A wagon carried him as far as Robineux, where he left it under a shed, for it would not have been prudent to risk it in the middle of the gorge. And he set off bravely, having to make nearly seven kilometers over the most abominable of roads. The route was otherwise of a wild beauty; it descended by continual turns between two enormous ledges of rock, so narrow in places that three men could not walk abreast. Farther on it skirted the precipices; the gorge opened abruptly; and one caught glimpses of the sea, of immense blue horizons. But M. Mouchel was not in a state of mind to admire the landscape. He swore as the pebbles rolled under his feet. It was the fault of Coqueville, he promised to shake up those donothings well. But, in the meantime, he was approaching. All at once, in the turning at the last rock, he saw the twenty houses of the village hanging to the flank of the cliff.

Nine o'clock struck. One would have believed it June, so blue and warm was the sky; a superb season, limpid air, gilded by the dust of the sun, refreshed by the good smell of the sea. M. Mouchel entered the only street of the village, where he came very often; and as he passed before Rouget's house, he went in. The house was empty. Then he cast his eye toward Fouasse's— Tupain's — Brisemotte's. Not a soul; all the doors open, and no one in the rooms. What did it mean? A light chill began to creep over his flesh. Then he thought of the authorities. Certainly, the Emperor would reassure him. But the Emperor's house was empty like the others. Even to the *garde champêtre,* there was failure! That village, silent and deserted, terrified him now. He ran to the Mayor's. There another surprise awaited him: the house was found in an abominable mess; they had not made the beds in three days; dirty dishes littered the place; chairs seemed to indicate a fight. His mind upset, dreaming of cataclysms, M. Mouchel determined to go on to the end, and he entered the church. No more curé than mayor. All the authorities, even religion itself had vanished. Coqueville abandoned, slept without a breath, without a dog, without a cat. Not even a fowl; the hens had taken themselves off. Nothing, a void, silence, a leaden sleep under the great blue sky.

Parbleu! It was no wonder that Coqueville brought no more fish! Coqueville had moved away. Coqueville was dead. He must notify the police. The mysterious catastrophe exalted

M. Mouchel, when, with the idea of descending to the beach, he uttered a cry. In the midst of the sands, the whole population lay stretched. He thought of a general massacre. But the sonorous snores came to undeceive him. During the night of Sunday, Coqueville had feasted so late that it had found itself in absolute inability to go home to bed. So it had slept on the sand, just where it had fallen, around the nine casks, completely empty.

Yes, all Coqueville was snoring there; I hear the children, the women, the old people, and the men. Not one was on his feet. There were some on their stomachs, there were some on their backs; others held themselves *en chien de fusils.*[3] As one makes his bed so must one lie on it. And the fellows found themselves, happen what may, scattered in their drunkenness like a handful of leaves driven by the wind. The men had rolled over, heads lower than heels. It was a scene full of good-fellowship; a dormitory in the open air; honest family folk taking their ease; for where there is care, there is no pleasure.

It was just at the new moon. Coqueville, thinking it had blown out its candle, had abandoned itself to the darkness. Then the day dawned; and now the sun was flaming, a sun which fell perpendicularly on the sleepers, powerless to make them open their eyelids. They slept rudely, all their faces beaming with the fine in-

[3] Primed for the event.

nocence of drunkards. The hens at early morning must have strayed down to peck at the casks, for they were drunk; they, too, sleeping on the sands. There were also five cats and five dogs, their paws in the air, drunk from licking the glasses glistening with sugar.

For a moment M. Mouchel walked about among the sleepers, taking care not to step on any of them. He understood, for at Grandport they, too, had received casks from the wreck of the English ship. All his wrath left him. What a touching and moral spectacle! Coqueville reconciled, the Mahés and the Floches sleeping together! With the last glass the deadliest enemies had embraced. Tupain and Fouasse lay there snoring, hand in hand, like brothers, incapable of coming to dispute a legacy. As to the Rouget household, it offered a still more amiable picture, Marie slept between Rouget and Brisemotte, as much as to say that henceforth they were to live thus, happy, all the three.

But one group especially exhibited a scene of family tenderness. It was Delphin and Margot; one on the neck of the other, they slept cheek to cheek, their lips still opened for a kiss. At their feet the Emperor, sleeping crosswise, guarded them. Above them La Queue snored like a father satisfied at having settled his daughter, while the Abbé Radiguet, fallen there like the others, with arms outspread, seemed to bless them. In her sleep Margot still extended her

151

rosy muzzle like an amorous cat who loves to have one scratch her under the chin.

The fête ended with a marriage. And M. Mouchel himself later married the Widow Dufeu, whom he beat to a jelly. Speak of that in Lower Normandy, they will tell you with a laugh, "Ah! yes, the fête at Coqueville!"

A WORK OF ART

THE STORY OF A GIFT

BY ANTON PAVLOVITCH CHEKHOV

A WORK OF ART

THE STORY OF A GIFT

BY ANTON PAVLOVITCH CHEKHOV

ALEXANDER SMIRNOFF, the only son of his mother, holding in his hand some object carefully wrapped in a newspaper, an angelic smile on his youthful face, entered the consulting-room of Dr. Koshelkoff.

"Ah, dear youth!" exclaimed the doctor, "how are you? What is the good news?"

Confused and excited, the young man replied:

"Doctor, my mother is sending her regards— I am her only son, you know— You saved my life. Your skill— We hardly know how to thank you!"

"Say no more, dear boy!" said the doctor, beaming with delight. "I have only done my duty. Anybody else would have done the same."

"I am the only son of my mother. We are poor, and, of course, can not repay you for your labors as you have deserved—and we feel it deeply. At the same time my mother—I am her only son, doctor—my mother humbly begs you to accept as a token of our gratitude a little

Translated by Archibald J. Wolfe. Copyright, 1905, by The Short Stories Co., Limited.

statuette she values very highly. It is a piece of antique bronze, and a rare work of art."

"My good fellow—" commenced the physician.

"No, doctor, you must not refuse," continued Alexander, unfolding his parcel. "You will deeply offend mother and myself, too. It is a little beauty. A rare antique. We have kept it in memory of father, who was a dealer in antique bronzes. My mother and myself continue the business."

Finally the youth succeeded in freeing his present from its wrappings, and placed it on the table with an air of great solemnity. It was a moderately tall candelabrum of antique bronze and of artistic workmanship. It represented two female figures somewhat scantily attired, and bearing an air of frivolity to describe which I have neither the required daring nor the temperament.

The figures smiled coquettishly, and looked as if they were ready to jump on the floor and to engage in some wild frolic, were they not restrained by the task of supporting the candle holder.

The doctor regarded his present for a few moments in silence, then scratched his head and coughed irresolutely.

"A beautiful article, to be sure," he finally said. "But you know—what shall I say? Why, it is hardly the thing, you know. Talk of *déshabille!* This is beyond the bounds of propriety. The devil!"

"W-w-why?"

"Now, how could I put a thing like that on my table? It will corrupt my residence."

"Doctor, you surprise me," answered Alexander, with an offended tone. "What queer views of art! This is a work of art! Look at it! What beauty, what delicacy of workmanship! It fills the soul with joy merely to look at it; it brings tears to one's eyes. Observe the movement, the atmosphere, the expression!"

"I fully appreciate it, my boy," interrupted the physician. "But you know I am a man of family. I have children. A mother-in-law. Ladies call here."

"Of course, if you look at it from the point of view of the common herd, you might regard it in a different light. But I beg of you, rise above the mob. Your refusal would hurt the feelings of my mother and of myself. I am her only son. You saved my life. We are asking you to accept something we hold very dear. I only deplore the fact that we have no companion piece to it."

"Thank you, dear fellow, and thank your mother. I see that I can not reason with you. But you should have thought of my children, you know, and the ladies. But I fear you will not listen to arguments."

"No use arguing, doctor," replied the grateful patient, made happy by the implied acceptance. "You put it right here, next to the Japanese vase. What a pity I have not the pair. What a pity!"

When his caller departed the doctor thoughtfully regarded his unwelcome present. He scratched his head and pondered.

"It is an exquisite thing, without doubt. It would be a pity to throw it into the street. It is quite impossible to leave it here, though. What a dilemma to be in. To whom could I give it? How to get rid of it?"

Finally he bethought himself of Ukhoff, a dear friend of his school days, and a rising lawyer, who had just successfully represented him in some trifling case.

"Good," said the doctor. "As a friend he refused to charge me a fee, and it is perfectly proper that I should make him a present. Besides, he is a single man and tremendously sporty."

Losing no time, the doctor carefully wrapped up the candlestick and drove to Ukhoff.

"There, old chap," he said to the lawyer, whom he happily found at home; "there I have come to thank you for that little favor. You refused to charge me a fee, but you must accept this present in token of my gratitude. Look—what a beauty!"

On seeing the present the attorney was transported with delight.

"This beats everything!" he fairly howled.

A WORK OF ART

"Hang it all, what inventive genius! Exquisite, immense. Where did you get such a little gem?"

Having expressed his delight, the lawyer anxiously looked at his friend and said:

"But you know, you must not leave this thing here. I can not accept it."

"Why?" gasped the doctor.

"You know my mother calls here, clients, too. Why, I would not dare to look my servants in the face. Take it away."

"Never! You must not refuse," exclaimed the physician with the energy of despair. "Look at the workmanship! Look at the expression! I will not listen to any refusals. I will feel insulted."

With these words the doctor hurried out of the house.

"A white elephant," the lawyer mumbled sadly, while the doctor, rubbing his hands with glee, drove home with an expression of relief.

The attorney studied his present at length and wondered what to do with it.

"It is simply delicious, but I can not keep it. It would be vandalism to throw it away, and the only thing to do is to give it away. But to whom?"

"I have it now," he fairly shouted. "The very thing, and how appropriate. I will take it to Shashkin, the comedian. The rascal is a connoisseur in such things. And this is the night of his jubilee."

In the evening the candelabrum, carefully

wrapped, was taken to Shashkin's dressing-room by a messenger boy. The whole evening that dressing-room was besieged by a crowd of men who came to view the present. An incessant roar of delight was kept up within, sounding like the joyous neighing of many horses. Whenever an actress approached the door leading to the sanctum, and curiously knocked, Shashkin's hoarse voice was heard in reply:

"No, my dear, you can't come in, I am not fully dressed."

After the performance Shashkin shrugged his shoulders and said:

"What on earth shall I do with this disreputable thing? My landlady would not tolerate it in the house. Here actresses call to see me. This is not a photograph, you can't hide it in the drawer."

The hair-dresser listened sympathetically while arranging the comedian's hair.

"Why don't you sell it?" he finally asked the actor. "A neighbor of mine, an old lady, deals in such things, and she will pay you a good price for it. An old woman by the name of Smirnoff, the whole town knows her."

Shashkin obeyed.

.   .   .   .

Two days later Dr. Koshelkoff sat peacefully in his study, enjoying his pipe and thinking of things medical, when suddenly the door of his room flew open, and Alexander Smirnoff burst

upon his sight. His face beamed with joy, he
fairly shone, and his whole body breathed inexpressible content.

In his hands he held an object wrapped in a
newspaper.

"Doctor," he began breathlessly, "imagine my
joy! What good fortune! Luckily for you my
mother has succeeded in obtaining a companion
piece to your candelabrum. You now have the
pair complete. Mother is so happy. I am her
only son, you know. You saved my life."

Trembling with joy and with excess of gratitude, young Smirnoff placed the candelabrum before the doctor. The physician opened his mouth,
attempted to say something, but the power of
speech failed him—and he said nothing.

THE BIT OF STRING

BY GUY DE MAUPASSANT

THE BIT OF STRING

BY GUY DE MAUPASSANT

ALONG all the roads leading to Goderville
the peasants and their wives were going
toward the town, for it was market-day.
The men walked at an easy pace, the whole
body thrown ahead at each movement of the
long, crooked legs, men deformed by rude labor,
by guiding the plow, which at once forces the
right shoulder upward and twists the waist; by
reaping, which spreads the knees, for solid foot-
ing; by all the patient and painful toil of the
country. Their blue blouses, glossy with starch,
as though varnished, ornamented at the neck and
wrists by a simple pattern in white, swelled out
round their bony chests, like captive balloons
from which heads, arms, and legs were protrud-
ing.

Some were leading by a cord a cow or calf,
and their wives behind the animals were hasten-
ing their pace by the strokes of branches stripped
of their leaves. The women carried on their
arms great baskets, out of which hung, here and
there, heads of chickens or ducks. They walked
with shorter steps than their husbands, and at a

Translated by Emar Soule. Copyright, 1899, by The Current Literature
Publishing Company.

more rapid pace, spare, erect and wrapped in scant shawls pinned across their flat chests, their heads enveloped in white linen drawn closely over the hair and surmounted by a bonnet.

Now a pleasure wagon passed at a jerky pony trot, shaking fantastically two men seated side by side, and a woman at the back of the vehicle, holding on to its sides to soften the hard jolts.

In the square of Goderville was a crowd—a jam of mingled human beings and beasts. The horns of cattle, the high hats of the rich farmers and the head-dresses of the women, emerged from the surface of the assembly; and discordant voices, clamorous, bawling, kept up a continuous and savage babel, overtopped now and then by a shout from the robust lungs of a merry countryman, or the lowing of a cow attached to the wall of a house. All this mass was redolent of the stable and soilure, of milk, of hay, of sweat, and diffused that rank, penetrating odor, human and bestial, peculiar to people of the fields.

Master Hauchecorne of Bréauté had just arrived at Goderville, and was going toward the square when he saw on the ground a bit of string. Master Hauchecorne, economist, like every true Norman, thought that anything might be of use worth picking up, and he bent down painfully, for he suffered from rheumatism. He took up the piece of string, and was winding it carefully, when he noticed Malandin, the harness-maker, watching him from his doorway. The two men had long ago had a quarrel about a halter, and both being vindictive, had remained unfriendly. Hauchecorne was seized with a kind of shame, at thus being seen by his enemy picking a bit of twine out of the mud. He quickly hid his prize under his blouse, then in his breeches pocket; then he pretended to search the ground again for something which he did not find, and he went off toward the market, his head in advance, bent double by his infirmities.

He was forthwith lost in the noisy, shuffling crowd everywhere in motion from innumerable buyings and sellings. The peasants examined the cows, went away, came back, hesitated, always fearful of being outwitted, never daring to decide, peering into the face of the vender, endlessly searching to discover the ruse in the man and the fault in the beast.

The women, putting their great baskets down at their feet, had drawn out their fowls, which were lying on the ground, legs bound, eyes wild, combs scarlet. They listened to offers, held to their prices unmoved, their faces inscrutable; or suddenly deciding to accept an offer, cried out to the would-be purchaser slowly moving away:

"Agreed, Master Hutine; I will give it at your price."

Then little by little the square emptied, and the Angelus sounding noon, those who lived too far to go home dispersed in the various public houses.

At Jourdain's the great dining-room was full
of feasters, as the vast court was full of vehicles
of every pedigree—carts, gigs, tilburies, pleasure
vans, carioles innumerable, yellow with mud,
mended, out of order, lifting to heaven their
shafts, like two arms, or nosing the ground, rear
in the air.

Opposite the tables of diners the great chim-
ney-piece, full of bright flame, threw a lively
warmth on the backs of the row at the right.
Three spits were turning, weighted with chickens, pigeons, and legs of mutton, and a delectable
odor of roast flesh and of juice streaming over
its golden brown skin, escaped from the hearth,
put every one in gay humor, and made mouths
water. All the aristocracy of the plow dined
there with Master Jourdain, innkeeper and horse-
dealer, a shrewd fellow, who had his dollars.

The platters were passed and emptied as were
the tankards of yellow cider. Each one talked of
his affairs, his purchases, his sales. The harvest
was discussed. The weather was good for grass,
but a little sharp for grain.

All at once the drum sounded in the court before the house. All save a few indifferent fellows
were quickly on their feet, and running to the
door or the windows, their mouths full, their napkins in their hands.

When he had finished his roulade the public
crier held forth in a jerky voice, cutting his
phrases at the wrong place:

THE BIT OF STRING

"It is made known to the inhabitants of Goderville and in general to all—the people present at market, that there was lost this morning, on the Benzeville road between—nine and ten o'clock, a wallet containing five hundred francs and important papers. You are asked to return —it to the town hall, without delay, or to the house of Master Fortuné Houlebrèque, of Manneville. There will be twenty francs reward."

Then the crier went on. One heard once more far off the muffled beating of his drum, and his voice enfeebled by the distance. Then they all began to talk of the event, estimating Master Houlebrèque's chances of finding or not finding his wallet.

And the meal went on.

They were finishing their coffee when the chief of police appeared at the door.

"Where is Master Hauchecorne of Bréauté?" he asked.

Hauchecorne, seated at the farther end of the table, replied:

"I'm here."

The chief proceeded:

"Master Hauchecorne, will you have the kindness to accompany me to the town hall? The mayor wishes to speak with you."

The countryman, surprised and disquieted, emptied at a draft his little glass of rum, arose, and, still more bent than in the morning, for the first movement after each relaxation was particularly difficult, he set out, repeating:

"I'm here, I'm here."

And he followed the chief.

The mayor was waiting for him, seated in his fauteuil. He was the notary of the vicinity, a big, solemn man, of pompous phrases.

"Master Hauchecorne," said he, "you were seen to pick up, on the Benzeville road, this morning, the wallet lost by Master Houlebrèque, of Manneville."

The peasant, astonished, looked at the mayor, frightened already, without knowing why, by this suspicion which had fallen on him.

"What! what! I picked up the wallet?"

"Yes; you yourself."

"Word of honor, I didn't even know of it."

"You were seen."

"Seen? What? Who saw me?"

"Monsieur Malandin, the harness-maker."

Then the old man remembered, understood, reddened with anger.

"He saw meh, th' lout? He saw meh pick up that string! See here, m'sieu mayor," and feeling in the bottom of his pocket, he drew out the bit of cord.

But the mayor, incredulous, shook his head.

"You won't make me believe, Master Hauchecorne, that Malandin, who is a man worthy of credence, took that thread for a wallet."

THE BIT OF STRING

The peasant, furious, raised his hand, spit, to attest his innocence, and declared:

"Yet it's the truth of God, the sacred truth, m'sieu mayor. On my soul and my salvation, I repeat it."

The mayor continued:

"After picking up the object you went on searching in the mud a long time to see if some piece of money mightn't have escaped you."

The old man gasped with indignation and fear.

"May one tell—may one tell lies like that to injure an honest man? May one say—"

His protest was vain. He was not believed. He was confronted with Monsieur Malandin, who repeated and sustained his former affirmation. For an hour the two men hurled insults at each other. Hauchecorne was searched, at his demand, and nothing was found on him. Finally the mayor, greatly perplexed, sent him away, warning him that he should inform the council and await orders.

The news spread. When he came out of the town hall the old man was surrounded and questioned with a curiosity serious or mocking, but with no ill-will in it.

He began to recount the story of the string, but no one believed him—they only laughed.

He went on, stopped by everybody, stopping his acquaintances, beginning anew his tale and his protestations, turning his pockets inside out to prove that he had nothing.

"Move on, old quibbler," they said to him.

And he became angry, exasperated, feverish, sick at heart, at not being believed. He did not know what to do, but told his story over and over.

Night came. It was time to go home. He set out with three of his neighbors, to whom he pointed out the place where he had picked up the bit of cord, and all the way home he talked of his adventure. In the evening he made a circuit of the village of Bréauté to tell it to everybody. He met only incredulity. He was ill all night from his trouble.

The next day, toward one o'clock in the afternoon, Marius Paumelle, a farm hand, of Ymanville, returned the wallet and its contents to Monsieur Houlebrèque, of Manneville. The man stated, in effect, that he had found the wallet in the road, but not knowing how to read, had taken it home to his employer.

The news spread all about. Master Hauchecorne was told of it. He at once set out again on his travels, and began to narrate his story, completed by the dénouement. He was triumphant.

"It's not the thing 'at grieved me most, you understand," he said, "but it's the lie. Nothing harms you like being charged with a lie."

All day long he talked of his adventure. He told it on the streets to men passing, in the taverns to men drinking, after church the next Sunday. He stopped strangers to tell it to them. Now he was tranquil, yet something half disturbed him, without his knowing exactly what. People had an amused air as they listened to him. They did not appear convinced. He thought he detected whispers behind his back.

Tuesday of the following week he betook himself to the market of Goderville, driven there by the need of exploiting his case. Malandin, standing in his doorway, began to laugh when he saw him passing. Why? He accosted a farmer of Criquetot, who did not let him finish, but giving him a blow in the pit of the stomach, cried in his face:

"Go your way, humbug!"

Master Hauchecorne was dumfounded, and more and more ill at ease. Why had he been called a humbug?

When he was seated at table in Jourdain's inn he again began to explain the affair. A jockey of Montivilliers cried to him:

"Come, come, old croaker, I know about your string!"

Hauchecorne stammered:

"But since it is found—the wallet?"

The other answered:

"Hold your tongue, father. One finds, another returns. I know nothing about it, but I implicate you."

The peasant was left choking. He understood

173

at last. He was accused of having returned the
wallet through an accomplice. He tried to protest. The whole table began to laugh. He could
not finish his dinner, and went out in the midst
of mockeries.

He returned home, ashamed and disgraced,
strangling with rage and confusion, so much the
more overwhelmed, in that he was capable, with
his Norman duplicity, of doing the very thing of
which he was accused, and even boasting of it as
a good stroke. Confusedly he saw his innocence
impossible to prove, his chicanery being well
known, and he felt himself cut to the heart by the
injustice of the suspicion.

Then he commenced again to recount his adventure, lengthening each day his story, adding
each time new reasonings, more energetic protestations, more solemn oaths, which he invented and
arranged in his hours of solitude, his mind occupied solely with the story of the string. He
was believed the less in proportion to the compli-
cation of his defense and the subtlety of his
argument.

"That's the reasoning of a liar," they said behind his back.

He felt it, spent himself, wore his life out in
useless efforts. He wasted away visibly. Wags
now made him tell "the string" for their amusement, as one makes a soldier who has fought recount his battle. His mind, harassed and unset-
tled, grew feeble.

THE BIT OF STRING

Toward the end of December he took to his bed. He died early in January, and in the delirium of his agony he attested his innocence, repeating:

"A little string . . . a little string . . . wait. here it is, m'sieu mayor!"

A SCANDAL IN BOHEMIA

BY A. CONAN DOYLE

A SCANDAL IN BOHEMIA

BY A. CONAN DOYLE

I

TO SHERLOCK HOLMES she is always *the* woman. I have seldom heard him mention her under any other name. In his eyes she eclipses and predominates the whole of her sex. It was not that he felt any emotion akin to love for Irene Adler. All emotions, and that one particularly, were abhorrent to his cold, precise, but admirably balanced mind. He was, I take it, the most perfect reasoning and observing machine that the world has seen; but as a lover, he would have placed himself in a false position. He never spoke of the softer passions, save with a gibe and a sneer. They were admirable things for the observer—excellent for drawing the veil from men's motives and actions. But for the trained reasoner to admit such intrusions into his own delicate and finely adjusted temperament was to introduce a distracting factor which might throw a doubt upon all his mental results. Grit in a sensitive instrument, or a crack in one of his own high-power lenses, would not be more disturbing than a strong emotion in a nature such as his. And yet there was but one woman to him, and that woman was the late Irene Adler, of dubious and questionable memory.

I had seen little of Holmes lately. My marriage had drifted us away from each other. My own complete happiness, and the home-centered interests which rise up around the man who first finds himself master of his own establishment, were sufficient to absorb all my attention; while Holmes, who loathed every form of society with his whole Bohemian soul, remained in our lodgings in Baker Street, buried among his old books, and alternating from week to week between cocaine and ambition, the drowsiness of the drug, and the fierce energy of his own keen nature. He was still, as ever, deeply attracted by the study of crime, and occupied his immense faculties and extraordinary powers of observation in following out those clews, and clearing up those mysteries, which had been abandoned as hopeless by the official police. From time to time I heard some vague account of his doings; of his summons to Odessa in the case of the Trepoff murder, of his clearing up of the singular tragedy of the Atkinson brothers at Trincomalee, and finally of the mission which he had accomplished so delicately and successfully for the reigning family of Holland. Beyond these signs of his activity, however, which I merely shared with all the readers of the daily press, I knew little of my former friend and companion.

One night—it was on the 20th of March,

A SCANDAL IN BOHEMIA

1888—I was returning from a journey to a patient (for I had now returned to civil practice), when my way led me through Baker Street. As I passed the well-remembered door, which must always be associated in my mind with my wooing, and with the dark incidents of the Study in Scarlet, I was seized with a keen desire to see Holmes again, and to know how he was employing his extraordinary powers. His rooms were brilliantly lighted, and even as I looked up, I saw his tall, spare figure pass twice in a dark silhouette against the blind. He was pacing the room swiftly, eagerly, with his head sunk upon his chest, and his hands clasped behind him. To me, who knew his every mood and habit, his attitude and manner told their own story. He was at work again. He had risen out of his drug-created dreams, and was hot upon the scent of some new problem. I rang the bell, and was shown up to the chamber which had formerly been in part my own.

His manner was not effusive. It seldom was; but he was glad, I think, to see me. With hardly a word spoken, but with a kindly eye, he waved me to an armchair, threw across his case of cigars, and indicated a spirit case and a gasogene in the corner. Then he stood before the fire, and looked me over in his singular introspective fashion.

"Wedlock suits you," he remarked. "I think, Watson, that you have put on seven and a half pounds since I saw you."

"Seven," I answered.

"Indeed, I should have thought a little more. Just a trifle more, I fancy, Watson. And in practice again, I observe. You did not tell me that you intended to go into harness."

"Then how do you know?"

"I see it, I deduce it. How do I know that you have been getting yourself very wet lately, and that you have a most clumsy and careless servant girl?"

"My dear Holmes," said I, "this is too much. You would certainly have been burned had you lived a few centuries ago. It is true that I had a country walk on Thursday and came home in a dreadful mess; but as I have changed my clothes, I can't imagine how you deduce it. As to Mary Jane, she is incorrigible, and my wife has given her notice; but there again I fail to see how you work it out."

He chuckled to himself and rubbed his long, nervous hands together.

"It is simplicity itself," said he; "my eyes tell me that on the inside of your left shoe, just where the firelight strikes it, the leather is scored by six almost parallel cuts. Obviously they have been caused by some one who has very carelessly scraped round the edges of the sole in order to remove crusted mud from it. Hence, you see, my double deduction that you had been out in vile weather, and that you had a particularly malignant boot-slicking specimen of the London slavey. As to your practice, if a gentleman walks into my rooms, smelling of iodoform, with a black mark of nitrate of silver upon his right forefinger, and a bulge on the side of his top-hat to show where he has secreted his stethoscope, I must be dull indeed if I do not pronounce him to be an active member of the medical profession."

I could not help laughing at the ease with which he explained his process of deduction. "When I hear you give your reasons," I remarked, "the thing always appears to me so ridiculously simple that I could easily do it myself, though at each successive instance of your reasoning I am baffled, until you explain your process. And yet, I believe that my eyes are as good as yours."

"Quite so," he answered, lighting a cigarette, and throwing himself down into an armchair. "You see, but you do not observe. The distinction is clear. For example, you have frequently seen the steps which lead up from the hall to this room."

"Frequently."

"How often?"

"Well, some hundreds of times."

"Then how many are there?"

"How many? I don't know?"

"Quite so! You have not observed. And yet you have seen. That is just my point. Now, I know there are seventeen steps, because I have both seen and observed. By the way, since you are interested in these little problems, and since you are good enough to chronicle one or two of my trifling experieneces, you may be interested in this." He threw over a sheet of thick pink-tinted note-paper which had been lying open upon the table. "It came by the last post," said he. "Read it aloud."

The note was undated, and without either signature or address.

"There will call upon you to-night, at 7:45 o'clock," it said, "a gentleman who desires to consult you upon a matter of the deepest moment. Your recent services to one of the royal houses of Europe have shown that you are one who may safely be trusted with matters which are of an importance which can hardly be exaggerated. This account of you we have from all quarters received. Be in your chamber, then, at that hour, and do not take it amiss if your visitor wears a mask."

"This is indeed a mystery," I remarked. "What do you imagine that it means?"

"I have no data yet. It is a capital mistake to theorize before one has data. Insensibly one begins to twist facts to suit theories, instead of theories to suit facts. But the note itself—what do you deduce from it?"

I carefully examined the writing, and the paper upon which it was written.

"The man who wrote it was presumably well to do," I remarked, endeavoring to imitate my

184

companion's processes. "Such paper could not be bought under half a crown a packet. It is peculiarly strong and stiff."

"Peculiar—that is the very word," said Holmes. "It is not an English paper at all. Hold it up to the light."

I did so, and saw a large *E* with a small *g*, a *P* and a large *G* with a small *t* woven into the texture of the paper.

"What do you make of that?" asked Holmes.

"The name of the maker, no doubt; or his monogram, rather."

"Not at all. The *G* with the small *t* stands for 'Gesellschaft,' which is the German for 'Company.' It is a customary contraction like our 'Co.' *P*, of course, stands for 'Papier.' Now for the *Eg*. Let us glance at our 'Continental Gazetteer.'" He took down a heavy brown volume from his shelves. "Eglow, Eglonitz—here we are, Egria. It is in a German-speaking country—in Bohemia, not far from Carlsbad. 'Remarkable as being the scene of the death of Wallenstein, and for its numerous glass factories and paper mills.' Ha! ha! my boy, what do you make of that?" His eyes sparkled, and he sent up a great blue triumphant cloud from his cigarette.

"The paper was made in Bohemia," I said.

"Precisely. And the man who wrote the note is a German. Do you note the peculiar construction of the sentence—'This account of you we have from all quarters received?' A Frenchman or

Russian could not have written that. It is the German who is so uncourteous to his verbs. It only remains therefore, to discover what is wanted by this German who writes upon Bohemian paper, and prefers wearing a mask to showing his face. And here he comes, if I am not mistaken, to resolve all our doubts."

As he spoke there was the sharp sound of horses' hoofs and grating wheels against the curb, followed by a sharp pull at the bell. Holmes whistled.

"A pair, by the sound," said he. "Yes," he continued, glancing out of the window. "A nice little brougham and a pair of beauties. A hundred and fifty guineas apiece. There's money in this case, Watson, if there is nothing else."

"I think I had better go, Holmes."

"Not a bit, doctor. Stay where you are. I am lost without my Boswell. And this promises to be interesting. It would be a pity to miss it."

"But your client——"

"Never mind him. I may want your help, and so may he. Here he comes. Sit down in that arm chair, doctor, and give us your best attention."

A slow and heavy step, which had been heard upon the stairs and in the passage, paused immediately outside the door. Then there was a loud and authoritative tap.

"Come in!" said Holmes.

A man entered who could hardly have been less than six feet six inches in height, with the chest and limbs of a Hercules. His dress was rich with a richness which would, in England, be looked upon as akin to bad taste. Heavy bands of astrakan were slashed across the sleeves and front of his double-breasted coat, while the deep-blue cloak which was thrown over his shoulders was lined with flame-colored silk, and secured at the neck with a brooch which consisted of a single flaming beryl. Boots which extended half way up his calves, and which were trimmed at the tops with rich brown fur, completed the impression of barbaric opulence which was suggested by his whole appearance. He carried a broad-brimmed hat in his hand, while he wore across the upper part of his face, extending down past the cheek bones, a black visard-mask, which he had apparently adjusted that very moment, for his hand was still raised to it as he entered. From the lower part of the face he appeared to be a man of strong character, with a thick, hanging lip, and a long, straight chin, suggestive of resolution pushed to the length of obstinacy.

"You had my note?" he asked, with a deep, harsh voice and a strongly marked German accent. "I told you that I would call." He looked from one to the other of us, as if uncertain which to address.

"Pray take a seat," said Holmes. "This is my friend and colleague, Dr. Watson, who is occasionally good enough to help me in my cases. Whom have I the honor to address?"

"You may address me as the Count von Kramm, a Bohemian nobleman. I understand that this gentleman, your friend, is a man of honor and discretion, whom I may trust with a matter of the most extreme importance. If not, I should much prefer to communicate with you alone."

I rose to go, but Holmes caught me by the wrist and pushed me back into my chair. "It is both, or none," said he. "You may say before this gentleman anything which you may say to me."

The count shrugged his broad shoulders. "Then I must begin," said he, "by binding you both to absolute secrecy for two years, at the end of that time the matter will be of no importance. At present it is not too much to say that it is of such weight that it may have an influence upon European history."

"I promise," said Holmes.

"And I."

"You will excuse this mask," continued our strange visitor. "The august person who employs me wishes his agent to be unknown to you, and I may confess at once that the title by which I have just called myself is not exactly my own."

"I was aware of it," said Holmes dryly.

"The circumstances are of great delicacy, and every precaution has to be taken to quench what might grow to be an immense scandal, and seriously compromise one of the reigning families of

Europe. To speak plainly, the matter implicates the great House of Ormstein, hereditary kings of Bohemia."

"I was also aware of that," murmured Holmes, settling himself down in his armchair, and closing his eyes.

Our visitor glanced with some apparent surprise at the languid, lounging figure of the man who had been, no doubt, depicted to him as the most incisive reasoner and most energetic agent in Europe. Holmes slowly reopened his eyes and looked impatiently at his gigantic client.

"If your majesty would condescend to state your case," he remarked, "I should be better able to advise you."

The man sprung from his chair, and paced up and down the room in uncontrollable agitation. Then, with a gesture of desperation, he tore the mask from his face and hurled it upon the ground.

"You are right," he cried, "I am the king. Why should I attempt to conceal it?"

"Why, indeed?" murmured Holmes. "Your majesty had not spoken before I was aware that I was addressing Wilhelm Gottsreich Sigismond von Ormstein, Grand Duke of Cassel-Felstein, and hereditary King of Bohemia."

"But you can understand," said our strange visitor, sitting down once more and passing his hand over his high, white forehead, "you can understand that I am not accustomed to doing such business in my own person. Yet the matter was so delicate that I could not confide it to an agent without putting myself in his power. I have come incognito from Prague for the purpose of consulting you."

"Then, pray consult," said Holmes, shutting his eyes once more.

"The facts are briefly these: Some five years ago, during a lengthy visit to Warsaw, I made the acquaintance of the well-known adventuress Irene Adler. The name is no doubt familiar to you."

"Kindly look her up in my index, doctor," murmured Holmes, without opening his eyes. For many years he had adopted a system for docketing all paragraphs concerning men and things, so that it was difficult to name a subject or a person on which he could not at once furnish information. In this case I found her biography sandwiched in between that of a Hebrew rabbi and that of a staff-commander who had written a monogram upon the deep-sea fishes.

"Let me see!" said Holmes. "Hum! Born in New Jersey in the year 1858. Contralto—hum! La Scala—hum! Prima-donna Imperial Opera of Warsaw—yes! Retired from operatic stage —ha! Living in London—quite so! Your majesty, as I understand, became entangled with this young person, wrote her some compromising letters, and is now desirous of getting those letters back."

"Precisely so. But how——"

"Was there a secret marriage?"

"None."

"No legal papers or certificates?"

"None."

"Then I fail to follow your majesty. If this young person should produce her letters for blackmailing or other purposes, how is she to prove their authenticity?"

"There is the writing."

"Pooh, pooh! Forgery."

"My private note-paper."

"Stolen."

"My own seal."

"Imitated."

"My photograph."

"Bought."

"We were both in the photograph."

"Oh, dear! That is very bad. Your majesty has indeed committed an indiscretion."

"I was mad—insane."

"You have compromised yourself seriously."

"I was only crown prince then. I was young, I am but thirty now."

"It must be recovered."

"We have tried and failed."

"Your majesty must pay. It must be bought."

"She will not sell."

"Stolen, then."

"Five attempts have been made. Twice

burglars in my pay ransacked her house. Once we diverted her luggage when she traveled. Twice she has been waylaid. There has been no result."

"No sign of it?"

"Absolutely none."

Holmes laughed. "It is quite a pretty little problem," said he.

"But a very serious one to me," returned the king reproachfully.

"Very, indeed. And what does she propose to do with the photograph?"

"To ruin me."

"But how?"

"I am about to be married."

"So I have heard."

"To Clotilde Lothman von Saxe-Meiningen, second daughter of the King of Scandinavia. You may know the strict principles of her family. She is herself the very soul of delicacy. A shadow of a doubt as to my conduct would bring the matter to an end."

"And Irene Adler?"

"Threatens to send them the photograph. And she will do it. I know that she will do it. You do not know her, but she has a soul of steel. She has the face of the most beautiful of women and the mind of the most resolute of men. Rather than I should marry another woman, there are no lengths to which she would not go— none."

"You are sure that she has not sent it yet?"

"I am sure."

"And why?"

"Because she has said that she would send it on the day when the betrothal was publicly proclaimed. That will be next Monday."

"Oh, then we have three days yet," said Holmes, with a yawn. "That is very fortunate, as I have one or two matters of importance to look into just at present. Your majesty will, of course, stay in London for the present?"

"Certainly. You will find me at the Langham, under the name of the Count von Kramm."

"Then I shall drop you a line to let you know how we progress."

"Pray do so; I shall be all anxiety."

"Then, as to money?"

"You have *carte blanche.*"

"Absolutely?"

"I tell you that I would give one of the provinces of my kingdom to have that photograph."

"And for present expenses?"

The king took a heavy chamois leather bag from under his cloak, and laid it on the table.

"There are three hundred pounds in gold, and seven hundred in notes," he said.

Holmes scribbled a receipt upon a sheet of his note-book, and handed it to him.

"And mademoiselle's address?" he asked.

"Is Briony Lodge, Serpentine Avenue, St. John's Wood."

Holmes took a note of it. "One other question," said he thoughtfully. "Was the photograph a cabinet?"

"It was."

"Then, good-night, your majesty, and I trust that we shall soon have some good news for you. And good-night, Watson," he added, as the wheels of the royal brougham rolled down the street. "If you will be good enough to call to-morrow afternoon, at three o'clock, I should like to chat this little matter over with you."

II

At three o'clock precisely I was at Baker Street, but Holmes had not yet returned. The landlady informed me that he had left the house shortly after eight o'clock in the morning. I sat down beside the fire, however, with the intention of awaiting him, however long he might be. I was already deeply interested in his inquiry, for, though it was surrounded by none of the grim and strange features which were associated with the two crimes which I have already recorded, still, the nature of the case and the exalted station of his client gave it a character of its own. Indeed, apart from the nature of the investigation which my friend had on hand, there was something in his masterly grasp of a situation, and his keen, incisive reasoning, which made it a pleasure to me to study his system of work, and to follow

the quick, subtle methods by which he disen-
tangled the most inextricable mysteries. So accustomed was I to his invariable success that the
very possibility of his failing had ceased to enter
into my head.

It was close upon four before the door opened,
and a drunken-looking groom, ill-kempt and
side-whiskered, with an inflamed face and disreputable clothes, walked into the room. Accustomed as I was to my friend's amazing powers
in the use of disguises, I had to look three times
before I was certain that it was indeed he. With
a nod he vanished into the bedroom, whence he
emerged in five minutes tweed-suited and respectable, as of old. Putting his hand into his
pockets, he stretched out his legs in front of the
fire, and laughed heartily for some minutes.

"Well, really!" he cried, and then he choked,
and laughed again until he was obliged to lie
back, limp and helpless, in the chair.

"What is it?"

"It's quite too funny. I am sure you could
never guess how I employed my morning, or what
I ended by doing."

"I can't imagine. I suppose that you have
been watching the habits, and, perhaps, the house
of Miss Irene Adler."

"Quite so, but the sequel was rather unusual.
I will tell you, however. I left the house a little
after eight o'clock this morning in the character
of a groom out of work. There is a wonderful

sympathy and freemasonry among horsy men. Be one of them, and you will know all that there is to know. I soon found Briony Lodge. It is a bijou villa, with a garden at the back, but built out in front right up to the road, two stories. Chubb lock to the door. Large sitting-room on the right side, well furnished, with long windows almost to the floor, and those preposterous English window-fasteners which a child could open. Behind there was nothing remarkable, save that the passage window could be reached from the top of the coach house. I walked round it and examined it closely from every point of view, but without noting anything else of interest.

"I then lounged down the street, and found, as I expected, that there was a mews in a lane which runs down by one wall of the garden. I lent the hostlers a hand in rubbing down their horses, and I received in exchange twopence, a glass of half-and-half, two fills of shag tobacco, and as much information as I could desire about Miss Adler, to say nothing of half a dozen other people in the neighborhood, in whom I was not in the least interested, but whose biographies I was compelled to listen to."

"And what of Irene Adler?" I asked.

"Oh, she has turned all the men's heads down in that part. She is the daintiest thing under a bonnet on this planet. So say the Serpentine Mews, to a man. She lives quietly, sings at concerts, drives out at five every day, and returns at seven sharp for dinner. Seldom goes out at other times, except when she sings. Has only one male visitor, but a good deal of him. He is dark, handsome, and dashing; never calls less than once a day, and often twice. He is a Mr. Godfrey Norton of the Inner Temple. See the advantages of a cabman as a confidant. They had driven him home a dozen times from Serpentine Mews, and knew all about him. When I had listened to all that they had to tell, I began to walk up and down near Briony Lodge once more, and to think over my plan of campaign.

"This Godfrey Norton was evidently an important factor in the matter. He was a lawyer. That sounded ominous. What was the relation between them, and what the object of his repeated visits? Was she his client, his friend, or his mistress? If the former, she had probably transferred the photograph to his keeping. If the latter, it was less likely. On the issue of this question depended whether I should continue my work at Briony Lodge, or turn my attention to the gentleman's chambers in the Temple. It was a delicate point, and it widened the field of my inquiry. I fear that I bore you with these details, but I have to let you see my little difficulties, if you are to understand the situation."

"I am following you closely," I answered.

"I was still balancing the matter in my mind, when a hansom cab drove up to Briony Lodge, and a gentleman sprung out. He was a remark-

ably handsome man, dark, aquiline, and mustached—evidently the man of whom I had heard.
He appeared to be in a great hurry, shouted to
the cabman to wait, and brushed past the maid,
who opened the door, with the air of a man who
was thoroughly at home.

"He was in the house about half an hour, and
I could catch glimpses of him in the windows of
the sitting room, pacing up and down, talking
excitedly and waving his arms. Of her I could
see nothing. Presently he emerged, looking even
more flurried than before. As he stepped up to
the cab, he pulled a gold watch from his pocket
and looked at it earnestly. 'Drive like the devil!'
he shouted, 'first to Gross & Hankey's in Regent
Street, and then to the Church of St. Monica in
the Edgeware Road. Half a guinea if you do it
in twenty minutes!'

"Away they went, and I was just wondering
whether I should not do well to follow them,
when up the lane came a neat little landau, the
coachman with his coat only half buttoned, and his
tie under his ear, while all the tags of his harness
were sticking out of the buckles. It hadn't
pulled up before she shot out of the hall door and
into it. I only caught a glimpse of her at the moment, but she was a lovely woman, with a face
that a man might die for.

" 'The Church of St. Monica, John,' she cried;
'and half a sovereign if you reach it in twenty
minutes.'

"This was quite too good to lose, Watson. I was just balancing whether I should run for it, or whether I should perch behind her landau, when a cab came through the street. The driver looked twice at such a shabby fare; but I jumped in before he could object. 'The Church of St. Monica,' said I, 'and half a sovereign if you reach it in twenty minutes.' It was 11:35, and of course it was clear enough what was in the wind.

"My cabby drove fast. I don't think I ever drove faster, but the others were there before us. The cab and landau with their steaming horses were in front of the door when I arrived. I paid the man, and hurried into the church. There was not a soul there save the two whom I had followed, and a surpliced clergyman, who seemed to be expostulating with them. They were all three standing in a knot in front of the altar. I lounged up the side aisle like any other idler who has dropped into a church. Suddenly, to my surprise, the three at the altar faced round to me, and Godfrey Norton came running as hard as he could toward me.

" 'Thank God!' he cried. 'You'll do. Come! Come!'

" 'What then?' I asked.

" 'Come, man, come; only three minutes, or it won't be legal.'

"I was half-dragged up to the altar, and, before I knew where I was, I found myself mumbling responses which were whispered in my ear, and vouching for things of which I knew nothing, and generally assisting in the secure tying up of Irene Adler, spinster, to Godfrey Norton, bachelor. It was all done in an instant, and there was the gentleman thanking me on the one side and the lady on the other, while the clergyman beamed on me in front. It was the most preposterous position in which I ever found myself in my life, and it was the thought of it that started me laughing just now. It seems that there had been some informality about their license; that the clergyman absolutely refused to marry them without a witness of some sort, and that my lucky appearance saved the bridegroom from having to sally out into the streets in search of a best man. The bride gave me a sovereign, and I mean to wear it on my watch chain in memory of the occasion."

"This is a very unexpected turn of affairs," said I; "and what then?"

"Well, I found my plans very seriously menaced. It looked as if the pair might take an immediate departure, and so necessitate very prompt and energetic measures on my part. At the church door, however, they separated, he driving back to the Temple, and she to her own house. 'I shall drive out in the park at five as usual,' she said, as she left him. I heard no more. They drove away in different directions and I went off to make my own arrangements."

"Which are?"

"Some cold beef and a glass of beer," he answered, ringing the bell. "I have been too busy to think of food, and I am likely to be busier still this evening. By the way, doctor, I shall want your co-operation."

"I shall be delighted."

"You don't mind breaking the law?"

"Not in the least."

"Nor running a chance of arrest?"

"Not in a good cause."

"Oh, the cause is excellent!"

"Then I am your man."

"I was sure that I might rely on you."

"But what is it you wish?"

"When Mrs. Turner has brought in the tray I will make it clear to you. Now," he said, as he turned hungrily on the simple fare that our landlady had provided, "I must discuss it while I eat, for I have not much time. It is nearly five now. In two hours we must be on the scene of action. Miss Irene, or madame, rather, returns from her drive at seven. We must be at Briony Lodge to meet her."

"And what then?"

"You must leave that to me. I have already arranged what is to occur. There is only one point on which I must insist. You must not interfere, come what may. You understand?"

"I am to be neutral?"

"To do nothing whatever. There will probably be some small unpleasantness. Do not join in it. It will end in my being conveyed into the house. Four or five minutes afterward the sitting-room window will open. You are to station yourself close to that open window."

"Yes."

"You are to watch me, for I will be visible to you."

"Yes."

"And when I raise my hand—so—you will throw into the room what I give you to throw, and will, at the same time, raise the cry of fire. You quite follow me?"

"Entirely."

"It is nothing very formidable," he said, taking a long, cigar-shaped roll from his pocket. It is an ordinary plumber's smoke-rocket, fitted with a cap at either end, to make it self-lighting. Your task is confined to that. When you raise your cry of fire, it will be taken up by quite a number of people. You may then walk to the end of the street, and I will rejoin you in ten minutes. I hope that I have made myself clear?"

"I am to remain neutral, to get near the window, to watch you, and, at the signal, to throw in this object, then to raise the cry of fire, and to wait you at the corner of the street."

"Precisely."

"Then you may entirely rely on me."

"That is excellent. I think, perhaps, it is almost time that I prepared for the new rôle I have to play."

He disappeared into his bedroom, and returned in a few minutes in the character of an amiable and simple-minded Nonconformist clergyman. His broad, black hat, his baggy trousers, his white tie, his sympathetic smile, and general look of peering and benevolent curiosity were such as Mr. John Hare alone could have equaled. It was not merely that Holmes changed his costume. His expression, his manner, his very soul seemed to vary with every fresh part that he assumed. The stage lost a fine actor, even as science lost an acute reasoner, when he became a specialist in crime.

It was 6:15 when we left Baker Street, and it still wanted ten minutes to the hour when we found ourselves in Serpentine Avenue. It was already dusk, and the lamps were just being lighted as we paced up and down in front of Briony Lodge, waiting for the coming of its occupant. The house was just such as I had pictured it from Sherlock Holmes' succinct description, but the locality appeared to be less private than I expected. On the contrary, for a small street in a quiet neighborhood, it was remarkably animated. There was a group of shabbily dressed men smoking and laughing in a corner, a scissors-grinder with his wheel, two guardsmen who were flirting with a nurse girl, and several well-dressed young men who were lounging up and down with cigars in their mouths.

"You see," remarked Holmes, as we paced to

and fro in front of the house, "this marriage rather simplifies matters. The photograph becomes a double-edged weapon now. The chances are that she would be as averse to its being seen by Mr. Godfrey Norton as our client is to its coming to the eyes of his princess. Now the question is—where are we to find the photograph?"

"Where, indeed?"

"It is most unlikely that she carries it about with her. It is cabinet size. Too large for easy concealment about a woman's dress. She knows that the king is capable of having her waylaid and searched. Two attempts of the sort have already been made. We may take it, then, that she does not carry it about with her."

"Where, then?"

"Her banker or her lawyer. There is that double possibility. But I am inclined to think neither. Women are naturally secretive, and they like to do their own secreting. Why should she hand it over to any one else? She could trust her own guardianship, but she could not tell what indirect or political influence might be brought to bear upon a business man. Besides, remember that she had resolved to use it within a few days. It must be where she can lay her hands upon it. It must be in her own house."

"But it has twice been burglarized."

"Pshaw! They did not know how to look."

"But how will you look?"

"I will not look."

"What then?"

"I will get her to show me."

"But she will refuse."

"She will not be able to. But I hear the rumble of wheels. It is her carriage. Now carry out my orders to the letter."

As he spoke, the gleam of the side-lights of a carriage came round the curve of the avenue. It was a smart little landau which rattled up to the door of Briony Lodge. As it pulled up one of the loafing men at the corner dashed forward to open the door in the hope of earning a copper, but was elbowed away by another loafer who had rushed up with the same intention. A fierce quarrel broke out, which was increased by the two guardsmen, who took sides with one of the loungers, and by the scissors-grinder, who was equally hot upon the other side. A blow was struck, and in an instant the lady, who had stepped from her carriage, was the centre of a little knot of struggling men who struck savagely at each other with their fists and sticks. Holmes dashed into the crowd to protect the lady; but, just as he reached her, he gave a cry and dropped to the ground, with the blood running freely down his face. At his fall the guardsmen took to their heels in one direction and the loungers in the other, while a number of better dressed people who had watched the scuffle without taking part in it crowded in to help the lady and to

attend to the injured man. Irene Adler, as I will
still call her, had hurried up the steps; but she
stood at the top, with her superb figure outlined
against the lights of the hall, looking back into
the street.

"Is the poor gentleman much hurt?" she asked.

"He is dead," cried several voices.

"No, no, there's life in him," shouted another.
"But he'll be gone before you can get him to the
hospital."

"He's a brave fellow," said a woman. "They
would have had the lady's purse and watch if it
hadn't been for him. They were a gang, and a
rough one, too. Ah! he's breathing now."

"He can't lie in the street. May we bring him
in, marm?"

"Surely. Bring him into the sitting room.
There is a comfortable sofa. This way, please."
Slowly and solemnly he was borne into Briony
Lodge, and laid out in the principal room, while
I still observed the proceedings from my post
by the window. The lamps had been lighted, but
the blinds had not been drawn, so that I could
see Holmes as he lay upon the couch. I do not
know whether he was seized with compunction
at that moment for the part he was playing, but
I know that I never felt more heartily ashamed
of myself in my life when I saw the beautiful
creature against whom I was conspiring, or the
grace and kindliness with which she waited upon
the injured man. And yet it would be the black-

est treachery to Holmes to draw back now from the part which he had intrusted to me. I hardened my heart, and took the smoke-rocket from under my ulster. After all, I thought, we are not injuring her. We are but preventing her from injuring another.

Holmes had sat upon the couch, and I saw him motion like a man who is in need of air. A maid rushed across and threw open the window. At the same instant I saw him raise his hand, and at the signal I tossed my rocket into the room with a cry of "Fire!" The word was no sooner out of my mouth than the whole crowd of spectators, well dressed and ill—gentlemen, hostlers, and servant-maids—joined in a general shriek of "Fire!" Thick clouds of smoke curled through the room, and out at the open window. I caught a glimpse of rushing figures, and a moment later the voice of Holmes from within assuring them that it was a false alarm. Slipping through the shouting crowd, I made my way to the corner of the street, and in ten minutes was rejoiced to find my friend's arm in mine, and to get away from the scene of uproar. He walked swiftly and in silence for some few minutes, until we had turned down one of the quiet streets which led toward the Edgware Road.

"You did it very nicely, doctor," he remarked. "Nothing could have been better. It is all right."

"You have the photograph?"

"I know where it is."

"And how did you find out?"

"She showed me, as I told you that she would."

"I am still in the dark."

"I do not wish to make a mystery," said he, laughing. "The matter was perfectly simple. You, of course, saw that every one in the street was an accomplice. They were all engaged for the evening."

"I guessed as much."

"Then, when the row broke out, I had a little moist red paint in the palm of my hand. I rushed forward, fell down, clapped my hand to my face, and became a piteous spectacle. It is an old trick."

"That also I could fathom."

"Then they carried me in. She was bound to have me in. What else could she do? And into her sitting room, which was the very room which I suspected. It lay between that and her bedroom, and I was determined to see which. They laid me on a couch, I motioned for air, they were compelled to open the window, and you had your chance."

"How did that help you?"

"It was all important. When a woman thinks that her house is on fire, her instinct is at once to rush to the thing which she values most. It is a perfectly overpowering impulse, and I have more than once taken advantage of it. In the case of the Darlington Substitution Scandal it was of use to me, and also in the Arnsworth Castle business. A married woman grabs at her baby—an unmarried one reaches for her jewel-box. Now it was clear to me that our lady of to-day had nothing in the house more precious to her than what we are in quest of. She would rush to secure it. The alarm of fire was admirably done. The smoke and shouting were enough to shake nerves of steel. She responded beautifully. The photograph is in a recess behind a sliding panel just above the right bell-pull. She was there in an instant, and I caught a glimpse of it as she half drew it out. When I cried out that it was a false alarm, she replaced it, glanced at the rocket, rushed from the room, and I have not seen her since. I rose, and, making my excuses, escaped from the house. I hesitated whether to attempt to secure the photograph at once; but the coachman had come in, and as he was watching me narrowly, it seemed safer to wait. A little overprecipitance may ruin all."

"And now?" I asked.

"Our quest is practically finished. I shall call with the king to-morrow, and with you, if you care to come with us. We will be shown into the sitting-room to wait for the lady, but it is probable that when she comes she may find neither us nor the photograph. It might be a satisfaction to his majesty to regain it with his own hands."

"And when will you call?"

"At eight in the morning. She will not be up, so that we shall have a clear field. Besides, we

must be prompt, for this marriage may mean a
complete change in her life and habits. I must
wire to the king without delay."

We had reached Baker Street, and had
stopped at the door. He was searching his
pockets for the key, when some one passing
said:

"Good-night, Mister Sherlock Holmes."

There were several people on the pavement at
the time, but the greeting appeared to come from
a slim youth in an ulster who had hurried by.

"I've heard that voice before," said Holmes,
staring down the dimly lighted street. "Now, I
wonder who the deuce that could have been?"

III

I slept at Baker Street that night, and we were
engaged upon our toast and coffee in the morning when the King of Bohemia rushed into the
room.

"You have really got it?" he cried, grasping
Sherlock Holmes by either shoulder, and looking
eagerly into his face.

"Not yet."

"But you have hopes?"

"I have hopes."

"Then come. I am all impatience to be gone."

"We must have a cab."

"No, my brougham is waiting."

"Then that will simplify matters." We descended, and started off once more for Briony Lodge.

"Irene Adler is married," remarked Holmes.

"Married! When?"

"Yesterday."

"But to whom?"

"To an English lawyer named Norton."

"But she could not love him."

"I am in hopes that she does."

"And why in hopes?"

"Because it would spare your majesty all fear of future annoyance. If the lady loves her husband, she does not love your majesty. If she does not love your majesty, there is no reason why she should interfere with your majesty's plan."

"It is true. And yet— Well, I wish she had been of my own station. What a queen she would have made!" He relapsed into a moody silence, which was not broken until we drew up in Serpentine Avenue.

The door of Briony Lodge was open, and an elderly woman stood upon the steps. She watched us with a sardonic eye as we stepped from the brougham.

"Mr. Sherlock Holmes, I believe?" said she.

"I am Mr. Holmes," answered my companion, looking at her with a questioning and rather startled gaze.

"Indeed! My mistress told me that you were likely to call. She left this morning, with her

husband, by the 5:15 train from Charing Cross,
for the Continent."

"What!" Sherlock Holmes staggered back,
white with chagrin and surprise.

"Do you mean that she has left England?"

"Never to return."

"And the papers?" asked the king hoarsely.
"All is lost!"

"We shall see." He pushed past the servant,
and rushed into the drawing room, followed by
the king and myself. The furniture was scattered
about in every direction, with dismantled shelves,
and open drawers, as if the lady had hurriedly
ransacked them before her flight. Holmes rushed
at the bell-pull, tore back a small sliding shutter,
and plunging in his hand, pulled out a photograph and a letter. The photograph was of Irene
Adler herself in evening dress; the letter was
superscribed to "Sherlock Holmes, Esq. To be
left till called for." My friend tore it open, and
we all three read it together. It was dated at
midnight of the preceding night, and ran in this
way:

"MY DEAR MR. SHERLOCK HOLMES: You really did it very well.
You took me in completely. Until after the alarm of the fire, I
had not a suspicion. But then, when I found how I had betrayed
myself, I began to think. I had been warned against you months
ago. I had been told that if the king employed an agent, it
would certainly be you. And your address had been given me.
Yet, with all this, you made me reveal what you wanted to know.
Even after I became suspicious, I found it hard to think evil of
such a dear, kind old clergyman. But, you know, I have been
trained as an actress myself. Male costume is nothing new to me.
I often take advantage of the freedom which it gives. I sent

A SCANDAL IN BOHEMIA

John, the coachman, to watch you, ran upstairs, got into my walking clothes, as I call them, and came down just as you departed.

"Well, I followed you to the door, and so made sure that I was really an object of interest to the celebrated Mr. Sherlock Holmes. Then I, rather imprudently, wished you good-night, and started for the Temple to see my husband.

"We both thought the best resource was flight, when pursued by so formidable an antagonist; so you will find the nest empty when you call to-morrow. As to the photograph, your client may rest in peace. I love and am loved by a better man than he. The king may do what he will without hindrance from one whom he has cruelly wronged. I keep it only to safeguard myself, and preserve a weapon which will always secure me from any steps which he might take in the future. I leave a photograph which he might care to possess; and I remain, dear Mr. Sherlock Holmes, very truly yours,

"IRENE NORTON, *née* ADLER."

"What a woman—oh, what a woman!" cried the King of Bohemia, when we had all three read this epistle. "Did I not tell you how quick and resolute she was? Would she not have made an admirable queen? Is it not a pity that she was not on my level?"

"From what I have seen of the lady, she seems, indeed, to be on a very different level to your majesty," said Holmes coldly. "I am sorry that I have not been able to bring your majesty's business to a more successful conclusion."

"On the contrary, my dear sir," cried the king, "nothing could be more successful. I know that her word is inviolate. The photograph is now as safe as if it were in the fire."

"I am glad to hear your majesty say so."

"I am immensely indebted to you. Pray tell me in what way I can reward you. This ring—" He slipped an emerald snake ring from his fin-

LOVE AND BREAD

BY JEAN AUGUST STRINDBERG

WHEN young Gustaf Falk, the assistant councilor, made his ceremonial proposal for Louise's hand to her father, the old gentleman's first question was: "How much are you earning?"

"Not more than a hundred kroner[1] a month. But Louise—"

"Never mind the rest," interrupted Falk's prospective father-in-law; "you don't earn enough."

"Oh, but Louise and I love each other so dearly! We are so sure of one another."

"Very likely. However, let me ask you: is twelve hundred a year the sum total of your resources?"

"We first became acquainted at Lidingö."

"Do you make anything beside your government salary?" persisted Louise's parent.

"Well, yes, I think we shall have sufficient. And then, you see, our mutual affection—"

"Yes, exactly; but let's have a few figures."

"Oh," said the enthusiastic suitor, "I can get enough by doing extra work!"

[1] A kroner is worth about twenty-eight cents.

"What sort of work? And how much?"

"I can give lessons in French, and also translate. And then I can get some proofreading."

"How much translation?" queried the elder, pencil in hand.

"I can't say exactly, but at present I am translating a French book at the rate of ten kroner per folio."

"How many folios are there altogether?"

"About a couple of dozen, I should say."

"Very well. Put this at two hundred and fifty kroner. Now, how much else?"

"Oh, I don't know. It's a little uncertain."

"What, you are not certain, and you intend to marry? You seem to have queer notions of marriage, young man! Do you realize that there will be children, and that you will have to feed and clothe them, and bring them up?"

"But," objected Falk, "the children may not come so very soon. And we love each other so dearly, that—"

"That the arrival of children may be prophesied quite safely." Then, relenting, Louise's father went on:

"I suppose you are both set on marrying, and I don't doubt but what you are really fond of each other. So it seems as though I should have to give my consent after all. Only make good use of the time that you are engaged to Louise by trying to increase your income."

Young Falk flushed with joy at this sanction,

and demonstratively kissed the old man's hand. Heavens, how happy he was—and his Louise, too! How proud they felt the first time they went out walking together arm in arm, and how everybody noticed the radiant happiness of the engaged couple!

In the evenings he came to see her, bringing with him the proof-sheets he had undertaken to correct. This made a good impression on papa, and earned the industrious young man a kiss from his betrothed. But one evening they went to the theatre for a change, and drove home in a cab, the cost of that evening's entertainment amounting to ten kroner. Then, on a few other evenings, instead of giving the lessons, he called at the young lady's house to take her for a little walk.

As the day set for the wedding drew near, they had to think about making the necessary purchases to furnish their flat. They bought two handsome beds of real walnut, with substantial spring mattresses and soft eiderdown quilts. Louise must have a blue quilt, as her hair was blond. They, of course, also paid a visit to the house-furnishers', where they selected a lamp with a red shade, a pretty porcelain statuette of Venus, a complete table service with knives, forks, and fine glassware. In picking out the kitchen utensils they were benefited by mama's advice and aid. It was a busy time for the assistant councilor—rushing about to find a house, looking after the workmen, seeing that all the furniture was got together, writing out checks, and what not.

Meanwhile it was perfectly natural that Gustaf could earn nothing extra. But when they were once married he would easily make it up. They intended to be most economical—only a couple of rooms to start with. Anyhow, you could furnish a small apartment better than a large one. So they took a first-floor apartment at six hundred kroner, consisting of two rooms, kitchen, and larder. At first Louise said she would prefer three rooms on the top landing. But what did it matter, after all, so long as they sincerely loved each other?

At last the rooms were furnished. The sleeping chamber was like a small sanctuary, the beds standing side by side like chariots taking their course along life's journey. The blue quilts, the snowy sheets, and the pillow-spreads embroidered with the young people's initials amorously intertwined, all had a bright and cheerful appearance. There was a tall, elegant screen for the use of Louise, whose piano—costing twelve hundred kroner—stood in the other chamber, which served as sitting-room, dining-room, and study, in one. Here, too, stood a large walnut writing-desk and dining-table, with chairs to match; a large gilt-framed mirror, a sofa, and a bookcase added to the general air of comfort and coziness.

The marriage ceremony took place on a Saturday night, and late on Sunday morning the happy young couple was still asleep. Gustaf rose first. Although the bright light of day was peering in through the shutters, he did not open them, but lit the red-shaded lamp, which threw a mysterious rosy glow over the porcelain Venus. The pretty young wife lay there languid and content; she had slept well, and had not been awakened— as it was Sunday—by the rumbling of early market wagons. Now the church bells were ringing joyfully, as if to celebrate the creation of man and woman.

Louise turned over, while Gustaf retired behind the screen to put on a few things. He went out into the kitchen to order lunch. How dazzlingly the new copper and tin utensils gleamed and glistened! And all was his own—his and hers. He told the cook to go to the neighboring restaurant, and request that the lunch be sent in. The proprietor knew about it; he had received full instructions the day before. All he needed now was a reminder that the moment had come.

The bridegroom thereupon returns to the bed-chamber and taps softly: "May I come in?"

A little scream is heard. Then: "No, dearest; just wait a minute!"

Gustaf lays the table himself. By the time the lunch arrives from the restaurant, the new plates and cutlery and glasses are set out on the fresh, white linen cloth. The bridal bouquet lies beside Louise's place. As she enters the room in her

embroidered morning wrapper, she is greeted by
the sunbeams. She still feels a little tired, so he
makes her take an armchair, and wheels it to the
table. A drop or two of liqueur enlivens her; a
mouthful of caviar stimulates her appetite.
Fancy what mama would say if she saw her
daughter drinking spirits! But that's the advantage of being married, you know; then you
can do whatever you please.

The young husband waits most attentively
upon his fair bride. What a pleasure, too! Of
course he has had good luncheons before, in his
bachelor days; but what comfort or satisfaction
had he ever derived from them? None. Thus he
reflects while consuming a plate of oysters and a
glass of beer. What numbskulls they are, those
bachelors, not to marry! And how selfish! Why,
there ought to be a tax on them, as on dogs.
Louise is not quite so severe, urging gently and
sweetly that perhaps the poor fellows who elect
the single state are subjects of pity. No doubt if
they could afford to marry, they would—she
thinks. Gustaf feels a slight pang at his heart.
Surely happiness is not to be measured by money.
No, no; but, but— Well, never mind, there will
soon be lots of work, and then everything will
run smoothly. For the present there is this delicious roast partridge with cranberry sauce to be
considered, and the Burgundy. These luxuries,
together with some fine artichokes, cause the
young wife a moment's alarm, and she timidly

asks Gustaf if they can afford living on such a scale. But Gustaf pours more wine into the glass of his little Louise, reassuring her and softening those groundless fears. "One day is not every day," he says; "and people ought to enjoy life when they can. Ah, how beautiful life is!"

At six o'clock an elegant carriage, with two horses, pulls up before the door, and the bridal pair take a drive. Louise is charmed as they roll along through the park, reclining there so comfortably, while they meet acquaintances on foot, who bow to them in obvious astonishment and envy. The assistant councilor has made a good match, they must think; he has chosen a girl with money. And they, poor souls, have to walk. How much pleasanter to ride, without effort, leaning against these soft cushions! It is symbolical of agreeable married life.

The first month was one of unceasing enjoyment—balls, parties, dinners, suppers, theatres. Still, the time they spent at home was really the best of all! It was a delightful sensation to carry Louise off home, from her parents, at night, when they would do as they pleased under their own roof. Arriving at the flat, they would make a little supper, and then they would sit comfortably, chatting until a late hour. Gustaf was all for economy—the theory of it, that is to say. One day the young bride and housekeeper tried smoked salmon with boiled potatoes. How she relished it, too! But Gustaf demurred, and when smoked salmon day came round again he invested in a brace of partridges. These he bought at the market for a kroner, exulting over the splendid bargain, of which Louise did not approve. She had once bought a pair for less money. Besides, to eat game was extravagant. However, it would not do to disagree with her husband about such a trifling matter.

After a couple of months more Louise Falk became strangely indisposed. Had she caught cold? Or had she perchance been poisoned by the metal kitchen utensils? The doctor who was called in merely laughed, and said it was all right —a queer diagnosis, to be sure, when the young lady was seriously ailing. Perhaps there was arsenic in the wall-paper. Falk took some to a chemist, biding him make a careful analysis. The chemist's report stated the wall-paper to be quite free from any harmful substance.

His wife's sickness not abating, Gustaf began to investigate on his own account, his studies in a medical book resulting in a certainty as to her ailment. She took warm foot-baths, and in a month's time her state was declared entirely promising. This was sudden—sooner than they had expected; yet how lovely to be papa and mama! Of course the child would be a boy—no doubt of that; and one must think of a name to give him. Meanwhile, though, Louise took her husband aside, and reminded him that since their marriage he had earned nothing to supplement his salary, which had proved far from sufficient. Well, it was true they had lived rather high, but now a change should be made, and everything would be satisfactory.

Next day the assistant councilor went to see his good friend the barrister, with a request that he indorse a promissory note. This would allow him to borrow the money that would be needed to meet certain unavoidable forthcoming expenses—as Falk made clear to his friend. "Yes," agreed the man of law, "marrying and raising a family is an expensive business. I have never been able to afford it."

Falk felt too much ashamed to press his request, and when he returned home, empty-handed, was greeted with the news that two strangers had been to the house, and had asked for him. They must be lieutenants in the army, thought Gustaf, friends belonging to the garrison of Fort Vaxholm. No, he was told, they could not have been lieutenants; they were much older-looking men. Ah, then they were two fellows he used to know in Upsala; they had probably heard of his marriage, and had come to look him up. Only the servant said they were not from Upsala, but were Stockholmers, and carried sticks. Mysterious—very; but no doubt they would come back.

Then the young husband went marketing again. He bought strawberries—at a bargain, of course.

"I will help you this once, but not again. I have little enough myself, and you are not my only child."

Delicacies must be provided for the mother, chicken and expensive wine. And the nurse has to be paid.

Fortunately, Falk's wife is soon on her feet again. She is like a girl once more, with a slender figure. Her pallor is quite becoming. Louise's father talks seriously to his son-in-law, however:

"Now, no more children, if you please, unless you want to be ruined."

For a brief space the junior Falk family continued to live on love and increasing debts. But one day bankruptcy knocked at the door. The seizure of the household effects was threatened. Then the old man came and took away Louise and her child, and as they rode off in a cab he made the bitter reflection that he had lent his girl to a young man, who had given her back after a year, dishonored. Louise would willingly have stayed with Gustaf, but there was nothing more to subsist upon. He remained behind, looking on while the bailiffs—those men with the sticks—denuded the flat of everything, furniture, bedding, crockery, cutlery, kitchen utensils, until it was stripped bare.

Now began real life for Gustaf. He managed to get a position as proofreader on a newspaper which was published in the morning, so that he had to work at his desk for several hours each night. As he had not actually been declared a bankrupt, he was allowed to keep his place in the government service, although he could hope for no more promotion. His father-in-law made the concession of letting him see his wife and child on Sundays, but he was never permitted to be alone with them. When he left, in the evening, to go to the newspaper office, they would accompany him to the gate, and he would depart in utter humiliation of soul. It might take him perhaps twenty years to pay off all his obligations. And then—yes, what then? Could he then support his wife and child? No, probably not. If, in the mean time, his father-in-law should die, they would be left without a home. So he must be thankful even to the hard-hearted old man who had so cruelly separated them.

Ah, yes, human life itself is indeed hard and cruel! The beasts of the field find maintenance easily enough, while of all created beings man alone must toil and spin. It is a shame, yes, it is a crying shame, that in this life everybody is not provided with gratuitous partridges and strawberries.

THE SUICIDE CLUB

STORY OF THE YOUNG MAN WITH THE
CREAM TARTS

BY ROBERT LOUIS STEVENSON

THE SUICIDE CLUB

STORY OF THE YOUNG MAN WITH THE CREAM TARTS

BY ROBERT LOUIS STEVENSON

DURING his residence in London, the accomplished Prince Florizel of Bohemia gained the affection of all classes by the seduction of his manner and by a well-considered generosity. He was a remarkable man even by what was known of him; and that was but a small part of what he actually did. Although of a placid temper in ordinary circumstances, and accustomed to take the world with as much philosophy as any plowman, the Prince of Bohemia was not without a taste for ways of life more adventurous and eccentric than that to which he was destined by his birth. Now and then, when he fell into a low humor, when there was no laughable play to witness in any of the London theatres, and when the season of the year was unsuitable to those field sports in which he excelled all competitors, he would summon his confidant and Master of the Horse, Colonel Geraldine, and bid him prepare himself against an evening ramble. The Master of the Horse was a young officer of a brave and even temerarious dispo-

"Mockery?" repeated Florizel. "And whom do you propose to mock?"

"I am not here to expound my philosophy," replied the other, "but to distribute these cream tarts. If I mention that I heartily include myself in the ridicule of the transaction, I hope you will consider honor satisfied and condescend. If not, you will constrain me to eat my twenty-eighth, and I own to being weary of the exercise."

"You touch me," said the Prince, "and I have all the will in the world to rescue you from this dilemma, but upon one condition. If my friend and I eat your cakes—for which we have neither of us any natural inclination—we shall expect you to join us at supper by way of recompense."

The young man seemed to reflect.

"I have still several dozen upon hand," he said at last; "and that will make it necessary for me to visit several more bars before my great affair is concluded. This will take some time; and if you are hungry—"

The Prince interrupted him with a polite gesture.

"My friend and I will accompany you," he said: "for we have already a deep interest in your very agreeable mode of passing an evening. And now that the preliminaries of peace are settled, allow me to sign the treaty for both."

And the Prince swallowed the tart with the best grace imaginable.

"It is delicious," said he.

"I perceive you are a connoisseur," replied the young man.

Colonel Geraldine likewise did honor to the pastry; and every one in that bar having now either accepted or refused his delicacies, the young man with the cream tarts led the way to another and similar establishment. The two commission-aires, who seemed to have grown accustomed to their absurd employment, followed immediately after; and the Prince and the Colonel brought up the rear, arm in arm, and smiling to each other as they went. In this order the company visited two other taverns, where scenes were enacted of a like nature to that already described—some re-fusing, some accepting, the favors of this vaga-bond hospitality, and the young man himself eat-ing each rejected tart.

On leaving the third saloon the young man counted his store. There were but nine re-maining, three in one tray and six in the other.

"Gentlemen," said he, addressing himself to his two new followers, "I am unwilling to delay your supper. I am positively sure you must be hungry. I feel that I owe you a special con-sideration. And on this great day for me, when I am closing a career of folly by my most con-spicuously silly action, I wish to behave hand-somely to all who give me countenance. Gentle-men, you shall wait no longer. Although my constitution is shattered by previous excesses, at the risk of my life I liquidate the suspensory condition."

With these words he crushed the nine remaining tarts into his mouth, and swallowed them at a single movement each. Then, turning to the commissionaires, he gave them a couple of sovereigns.

"I have to thank you," said he, "for your extraordinary patience."

And he dismissed them with a bow apiece. For some seconds he stood looking at the purse from which he had just paid his assistants, then, with a laugh, he tossed it into the middle of the street, and signified his readiness for supper.

In a small French restaurant in Soho, which had enjoyed an exaggerated reputation for some little while, but had already begun to be forgotten, and in a private room up two pair of stairs, the three companions made a very elegant supper, and drank three or four bottles of champagne, talking the while upon indifferent subjects. The young man was fluent and gay, but he laughed louder than was natural in a person of polite breeding; his hands trembled violently, and the voice took sudden and surprising inflections, which seemed to be independent of his will. The dessert had been cleared away, and all three had lighted their cigars, when the Prince addressed him in these words:—

"You will, I am sure, pardon my curiosity. What I have seen of you has greatly pleased but

even more puzzled me. And though I should be
loath to seem indiscreet, I must tell you that my
friend and I are persons very well worthy to be
entrusted with a secret. We have many of our
own, which we are continually revealing to improper ears. And if, as I suppose, your story is
a silly one, you need have no delicacy with us,
who are two of the silliest men in England. My
name is Godall, Theophilus Godall; my friend is
Major Alfred Hammersmith—or at least, such
is the name by which he chooses to be known. We
pass our lives entirely in the search for extravagant adventures; and there is no extravagance
with which we are not capable of sympathy."

"I like you, Mr. Godall," returned the young
man; "you inspire me with a natural confidence;
and I have not the slightest objection to our
friend, the Major; whom I take to be a nobleman in masquerade. At least, I am sure he is
no soldier."

The Colonel smiled at this compliment to the
perfection of his art; and the young man went on
in a more animated manner.

"There is every reason why I should not tell
you my story. Perhaps that is just the reason
why I am going to do so. At least, you seem so
well prepared to hear a tale of silliness that I
can not find it in my heart to disappoint you.
My name, in spite of your example, I shall keep
to myself. My age is not essential to the narrative. I am descended from my ancestors by

ordinary generation, and from them I inherited
the very eligible human tenement which I still oc-
cupy and a fortune of three hundred pounds a
year. I suppose they also handed on to me a
hare-brain humor, which it has been my chief delight to indulge. I received a good education. I
can play the violin nearly well enough to earn
money in the orchestra of a penny gaff, but not
quite. The same remark applies to the flute and
the French horn. I learned enough of whist to
lose about a hundred a year at that scientific
game. My acquaintance with French was sufficient to enable me to squander money in Paris
with almost the same facility as in London. In
short, I am a person full of manly accomplish-
ments. I have had every sort of adventure, in-
cluding a duel about nothing. Only two months
ago I met a young lady exactly suited to my
taste in mind and body; I found my heart melt; I
saw that I had come upon my fate at last, and
was in the way to fall in love. But when I came
to reckon up what remained to me of my capital,
I found it amounted to something less than four
hundred pounds! I ask you fairly—can a man
who respects himself fall in love on four hundred
pounds? I concluded, certainly not; left the
presence of my charmer, and slightly accelerat-
ing my usual rate of expenditure, came this morning to my last eighty pounds. This I divided
into two equal parts; forty I reserved for a particular purpose; the remaining forty I was to

dissipate before the night. I have passed a very entertaining day, and played many farces besides that of the cream tarts which procured me the advantage of your acquaintance; for I was determined, as I told you, to bring a foolish career to a still more foolish conclusion; and when you saw me throw my purse into the street, the forty pounds were at an end. Now you know me as well as I know myself: a fool, but consistent in his folly; and, as I will ask you to believe, neither a whimperer nor a coward."

From the whole tone of the young man's statement it was plain that he harbored very bitter and contemptuous thoughts about himself. His auditors were led to imagine that his love affair was nearer his heart than he admitted, and that he had a design on his own life. The farce of the cream tarts began to have very much the air of a tragedy in disguise.

"Why, is this not odd," broke out Geraldine, giving a look to Prince Florizel, "that we three fellows should have met by the merest accident in so large a wilderness as London, and should be so nearly in the same condition?"

"How?" cried the young man. "Are you, too, ruined? Is this supper a folly like my cream tarts? Has the devil brought three of his own together for a last carouse?"

"The devil, depend upon it, can sometimes do a very gentlemanly thing," returned Prince Florizel; "and I am so much touched by this coincidence, that, although we are not entirely in the same case, I am going to put an end to the disparity. Let your heroic treatment of the last cream tarts be my example."

So saying, the Prince drew out his purse and took from it a small bundle of bank-notes.

"You see, I was a week or so behind you, but I mean to catch you up and come neck and neck into the winning-post," he continued. "This," laying one of the notes upon the table, "will suffice for the bill. As for the rest——"

He tossed them into the fire, and they went up the chimney in a single blaze.

The young man tried to catch his arm, but as the table was between them his interference came too late.

"Unhappy man," he cried, "you should not have burned them all! You should have kept forty pounds."

"Forty pounds!" repeated the Prince. "Why, in Heaven's name, forty pounds?"

"Why not eighty?" cried the Colonel; "for to my certain knowledge there must have been a hundred in the bundle."

"It was only forty pounds he needed," said the young man gloomily. "But without them there is no admission. The rule is strict. Forty pounds for each. Accursed life, where a man can not even die without money!"

The Prince and the Colonel exchanged glances.

"Explain yourself," said the latter. "I have still a pocket-book tolerably well lined, and I need not say how readily I would share my wealth with Godall. But I must know to what end: you must certainly tell us what you mean."

The young man seemed to awaken; he looked uneasily from one to the other, and his face flushed deeply.

"You are not fooling me?" he asked. "You are indeed ruined men like me?"

"Indeed, I am for my part," replied the Colonel.

"And for mine," said the Prince, "I have given you proof. Who but a ruined man would throw his notes into the fire? The action speaks for itself."

"A ruined man—yes," returned the other suspiciously, "or else a millionaire."

"Enough, sir," said the Prince; "I have said so, and I am not accustomed to have my word remain in doubt."

"Ruined?" said the young man. "Are you ruined, like me? Are you, after a life of indulgence, come to such a pass that you can only indulge yourself in one thing more? Are you"— he kept lowering his voice as he went on—"are you going to give yourself that last indulgence! Are you going to avoid the consequences of your folly by the one infallible and easy path? Are you going to give the slip to the sheriff's officers of conscience by the one open door?"

Suddenly he broke off and attempted to laugh.

"Here is your health!" he cried, emptying his glass, "and good night to you, my merry ruined men."

Colonel Geraldine caught him by the arm as he was about to rise.

"You lack confidence in us," he said, "and you are wrong. To all your questions I make answer in the affirmative. But I am not so timid, and can speak the Queen's English plainly. We too, like yourself, have had enough of life, and are determined to die. Sooner or later, alone or together, we mean to seek out death and beard him where he lies ready. Since we have met you, and your case is more pressing, let it be to-night—and at once—and, if you will, all three together. Such a penniless trio," he cried, "should go arm in arm into the hall of Pluto, and give each other some countenance among the shades!"

Geraldine had hit exactly on the manners and intonations that became the part he was playing. The Prince himself was disturbed, and looked over at his confidant with a shade of doubt. As for the young man, the flush came back darkly into his cheek, and his eyes threw out a spark of light.

"You are the men for me!" he cried, with an almost terrible gaiety. "Shake hands upon the bargain!" (his hand was cold and wet). "You little know in what a company you will begin the march! You little know in what a happy moment for yourselves you partook of my cream tarts! I am only a unit, but I am a unit in an army. I know Death's private door. I am one of his familiars, and can show you into eternity without ceremony and yet without scandal."

They called upon him eagerly to explain his meaning.

"Can you muster eighty pounds between you?" he demanded.

Geraldine ostentatiously consulted his pocket-book, and replied in the affirmative.

"Fortunate beings!" cried the young man. "Forty pounds is the entry money of the Suicide Club."

"The Suicide Club," said the Prince, "why, what the devil is that?"

"Listen," said the young man; "this is the age of conveniences, and I have to tell you of the last perfection of the sort. We have affairs in different places; and hence railways were invented. Railways separated us infallibly from our friends; and so telegraphs were made that we might communicate speedily at great distances. Even in hotels we have lifts to spare us a climb of some hundred steps. Now, we know that life is only a stage to play the fool upon as long as the part amuses us. There was one more convenience lacking to modern comfort; a decent, easy way to quit that stage; the back stairs to liberty; or, as I said this moment, Death's private door. This, my two fellow-rebels, is supplied by the Suicide Club. Do not suppose that you and I are alone, or even exceptional, in the highly reasonable desire that we profess. A large number of our fellowmen, who have grown heartily sick of the performance in which they are expected to join daily and all their lives long, are only kept from flight by one or two considerations. Some have families who would be shocked, or even blamed, if the matter became public; others have a weakness at heart and recoil from the circumstances of death. That is, to some extent, my own experience. I can not put a pistol to my head and draw the trigger; for something stronger than myself withholds the act; and although I loathe life, I have not strength enough in my body to take hold of death and be done with it. For such as I, and for all who desire to be out of the coil without posthumous scandal, the Suicide Club has been inaugurated. How this has been managed, what is its history, or what may be its ramifications in other lands, I am myself uninformed; and what I know of its constitution, I am not at liberty to communicate to you. To this extent, however, I am at your service. If you are truly tired of life, I will introduce you to-night to a meeting; and if not to-night, at least some time within the week, you will be easily relieved of your existences. It is now (consulting his watch) eleven; by half-past, at latest, we must leave this place; so that you have half an hour before you to consider my proposal. It is more serious than a cream tart," he added, with a smile; "and I suspect more palatable."

"More serious, certainly," returned Colonel Geraldine; "and as it is so much more so, will you allow me five minutes' speech in private with my friend, Mr. Godall?"

"It is only fair," answered the young man. "If you will permit, I will retire."

"You will be very obliging," said the Colonel.

As soon as the two were alone—"What," said Prince Florizel, "is the use of this confabulation, Geraldine? I see you are flurried, whereas my mind is very tranquilly made up. I will see the end of this."

"Your Highness," said the Colonel turning pale; "let me ask you to consider the importance of your life, not only to your friends, but to the public interest. 'If not to-night,' said this madman; but supposing that to-night some irreparable disaster were to overtake your Highness's person, what, let me ask you, what would be my despair, and what the concern and disaster of a great nation?"

"I will see the end of this," repeated the Prince in his most deliberate tones; "and have the kindness, Colonel Geraldine, to remember and respect your word of honor as a gentleman. Under no circumstances, recollect, nor without my special authority, are you to betray the incognito under which I choose to go abroad. These were my commands, which I now reiterate. And now," he added, "let me ask you to call for the bill."

Colonel Geraldine bowed in submission; but he had a very white face as he summoned the young man of the cream tarts, and issued his directions to the waiter. The Prince preserved his undisturbed demeanor, and described a Palais Royal farce to the young suicide with great humor and gusto. He avoided the Colonel's appealing looks without ostentation, and selected another cheroot with more than usual care. Indeed, he was now the only man of the party who kept any command over his nerves.

The bill was discharged, the Prince giving the whole change of the note to the astonished waiter; and the three drove off in a four wheeler. They were not long upon the way before the cab stopped at the entrance to a rather dark court. Here all descended.

After Geraldine had paid the fare, the young man turned, and addressed Prince Florizel as follows:

"It is still time, Mr. Godall, to make good your escape into thraldom. And for you too, Major Hammersmith. Reflect well before you take another step; and if your hearts say no— here are the crossroads."

"Lead on, sir," said the Prince. "I am not the man to go back from a thing once said."

"Your coolness does me good," replied their guide. "I have never seen any one so unmoved at this conjuncture; and yet you are not the first whom I have escorted to this door. More than one of my friends has preceded me, where I knew I must shortly follow. But this is of no interest to you. Wait me here for only a few moments; I shall return as soon as I have arranged the preliminaries of your introduction."

And with that the young man, waving his hand to his companions, turned into the court, entered a doorway and disappeared.

"Of all our follies," said Colonel Geraldine in a low voice, "this is the wildest and most dangerous."

"I perfectly believe so," returned the Prince.

"We have still," pursued the Colonel, "a moment to ourselves. Let me beseech your Highness to profit by the opportunity and retire. The consequences of this step are so dark, and may be so grave, that I feel myself justified in pushing a little farther than usual the liberty which your Highness is so condescending as to allow me in private."

"Am I to understand that Colonel Geraldine is afraid?" asked his Highness, taking his cheroot from his lips, and looking keenly into the other's face.

"My fear is certainly not personal," replied the other proudly; "of that your Highness may rest well assured."

"I had supposed as much," returned the Prince, with undisturbed good-humor; "but I was unwilling to remind you of the difference in our stations. No more—no more," he added, seeing Geraldine about to apologize, "you stand excused."

And he smoked placidly, leaning against a railing, until the young man returned.

"Well," he asked, "has our reception been arranged?"

"Follow me," was the reply. "The President will see you in the cabinet. And let me warn you to be frank in your answers. I have stood your guarantee; but the club requires a searching inquiry before admission; for the indiscretion of a single member would lead to the dispersion of the whole society forever."

The Prince and Geraldine put their heads together for a moment. "Bear me out in this," said the one; and "bear me out in that," said the other; and by boldly taking up the characters of men with whom both were acquainted, they had come to an agreement in a twinkling, and were ready to follow their guide into the President's cabinet.

There were no formidable obstacles to pass. The outer door stood open; the door of the cabinet was ajar; and there, in a small but very high apartment, the young man left them once more.

"He will be here immediately," he said with a nod, as he disappeared.

Voices were audible in the cabinet through the folding doors which formed one end; and now and then the noise of a champagne cork, followed by a burst of laughter, intervened among the sounds of conversation. A single tall window looked out upon the river and the embankment; and by the disposition of the lights they judged themselves not far from Charing Cross station. The furniture was scanty, and the coverings worn to the thread; and there was nothing movable except a hand-bell in the center of a round table, and the hats and coats of a considerable party hung round the wall on pegs.

"What sort of a den is this?" said Geraldine.

"That is what I have come to see," replied the Prince. "If they keep live devils on the premises, the thing may grow amusing."

Just then the folding door was opened no more than necessary for the passage of a human body; and there entered at the same moment a louder buzz of talk, and the redoubtable President of the Suicide Club. The President was a man of fifty or upward; large and rambling in his gait, with shaggy side-whiskers, a bald top to his head, and a veiled gray eye, which now and then emitted a twinkle. His mouth, which embraced a large cigar, he kept continually screwing round and round and from side to side, as he looked sagaciously and coldly at the strangers. He was dressed in light tweeds, with his neck very open, in a striped shirt collar; and carried a minute book under one arm.

"Good evening," said he, after he had closed

the door behind him. "I am told you wish to speak with me."

"We have a desire, sir, to join the Suicide Club," replied the Colonel.

The President rolled his cigar about in his mouth.

"What is that?" he said abruptly.

"Pardon me," returned the Colonel, "but I believe you are the person best qualified to give us information on that point."

"I?" cried the President. "A Suicide Club? Come, come! this is a frolic for All Fools' Day. I can make allowances for gentlemen who get merry in the liquor; but let there be an end to this."

"Call your Club what you will," said the Colonel, "you have some company behind these doors, and we insist on joining it."

"Sir," returned the President, curtly, "you have made a mistake. This is a private house, and you must leave it instantly."

The Prince had remained quietly in his seat throughout this little colloquy; but now, when the Colonel looked over to him, as much as to say, "Take your answer and come away, for God's sake!" he drew his cheroot from his mouth, and spoke:

"I have come here," said he, "upon the invitation of a friend of yours. He has doubtless informed you of my intention in thus intruding on your party. Let me remind you that a person in my circumstances has exceedingly little to bind him, and is not at all likely to tolerate much rudeness. I am a very quiet man, as a usual thing; but, my dear sir, you are either going to oblige me in the little matter of which you are aware, or you shall very bitterly repent that you ever admitted me to your ante-chamber."

The President laughed aloud.

"That is the way to speak," said he. "You are a man who is a man. You know the way to my heart, and can do what you like with me. Will you," he continued, addressing Geraldine, "will you step aside for a few minutes? I shall finish first with your companion, and some of the club's formalities require to be fulfilled in private."

With these words he opened the door of a small closet, into which he shut the Colonel.

"I believe in you," he said to Florizel, as soon as they were alone; "but are you sure of your friend?"

"Not so sure as I am of myself, though he has more cogent reasons," answered Florizel, "but sure enough to bring him here without alarm. He has had enough to cure the most tenacious man of life. He was cashiered the other day for cheating at cards."

"A good reason, I daresay," replied the President; "at least, we have another in the same case, and I feel sure of him. Have you also been in the Service, may I ask?"

"I have," was the reply; "but I was too lazy, I left it early."

"What is your reason for being tired of life?" pursued the President.

"The same, as near as I can make out," answered the Prince; "unadulterated laziness."

The President started. "D——n it," said he, "you must have something better than that."

"I have no more money," added Florizel. "That is also a vexation, without doubt. It brings my sense of idleness to an acute point."

The President rolled his cigar round in his mouth for some seconds, directing his gaze straight into the eyes of this unusual neophyte; but the Prince supported his scrutiny with unabashed good temper.

"If I had not a deal of experience," said the President at last, "I should turn you off. But I know the world; and this much any way, that the most frivolous excuses for a suicide are often the toughest to stand by. And when I downright like a man, as I do you, sir, I would rather strain the regulation than deny him."

The Prince and the Colonel, one after the other, were subjected to a long and particular interrogatory: the Prince alone; but Geraldine in the presence of the Prince, so that the President might observe the countenance of the one while the other was being warmly cross-examined. The result was satisfactory; and the President, after having booked a few details of each case, produced a form of oath to be accepted. Nothing could be conceived more passive than the obedience promised, or more stringent than the terms by which the juror bound himself. The man who forfeited a pledge so awful could scarcely have a rag of honor or any of the consolations of religion left to him. Florizel signed the document, but not without a shudder; the Colonel followed his example with an air of great depression. Then the President received the entry money; and without more ado, introduced the two friends into the smoking-room of the Suicide Club.

The smoking-room of the Suicide Club was the same height as the cabinet into which it opened, but much larger, and papered from top to bottom with an imitation of oak wainscot. A large and cheerful fire and a number of gas-jets illuminated the company. The Prince and his follower made the number up to eighteen. Most of the party were smoking, and drinking champagne; a feverish hilarity reigned, with sudden and rather ghastly pauses.

"Is this a full meeting?" asked the Prince.

"Middling," said the President. "By the way," he added, "if you have any money, it is usual to offer some champagne. It keeps up a good spirit, and is one of my own little perquisites."

"Hammersmith," said Florizel, "I may leave the champagne to you."

"For my part," said a second, "I wish no more than a bandage for my eyes and cotton for my ears. Only they have no cotton thick enough in this world."

A third was for reading the mysteries of life in a future state; and a fourth professed that he would never have joined the club, if he had not been induced to believe in Mr. Darwin.

"I could not bear," said this remarkable suicide, "to be descended from an ape."

Altogether, the Prince was disappointed by the bearing and conversation of the members.

"It does not seem to me," he thought, "a matter for so much disturbance. If a man has made up his mind to kill himself, let him do it, in God's name, like a gentleman. This flutter and big talk is out of place."

In the meanwhile Colonel Geraldine was a prey to the blackest apprehensions; the club and its rules were still a mystery, and he looked round the room for some one who should be able to set his mind at rest. In this survey his eye lighted on the paralytic person with the strong spectacles; and seeing him so exceedingly tranquil, he besought the President, who was going in and out of the room under a pressure of business, to present him to the gentleman on the divan.

The functionary explained the needlessness of all such formalities within the club, but nevertheless presented Mr. Hammersmith to Mr. Malthus.

THE SUICIDE CLUB

Mr. Malthus looked at the Colonel curiously, and then requested him to take a seat upon his right.

"You are a newcomer," he said, "and wish information? You have come to the proper source. It is two years since I first visited this charming club."

The Colonel breathed again. If Mr. Malthus had frequented the place for two years there could be little danger for the Prince in a single evening. But Geraldine was none the less astonished, and began to suspect a mystification.

"What!" cried he, "two years! I thought—but indeed I see I have been made the subject of a pleasantry."

"By no means," replied Mr. Malthus mildly. "My case is peculiar. I am not, properly speaking, a suicide at all; but, as it were, an honorary member. I rarely visit the club twice in two months. My infirmity and the kindness of the President have procured me these little immunities, for which besides I pay at an advanced rate. Even as it is my luck has been extraordinary."

"I am afraid," said the Colonel, "that I must ask you to be more explicit. You must remember that I am still most imperfectly acquainted with the rules of the club."

"An ordinary member who comes here in search of death like yourself," replied the paralytic, "returns every evening until fortune favors him.

He can, even if he is penniless, get board and lodging from the President: very fair, I believe, and clean, although, of course, not luxurious; that could hardly be, considering the exiguity (if I may so express myself) of the subscription. And then the President's company is a delicacy in itself."

"Indeed!" cried Geraldine, "he had not greatly prepossessed me."

"Ah!" said Mr. Malthus, "you do not know the man: the drollest fellow! What stories! What cynicism! He knows life to admiration and, between ourselves, is probably the most corrupt rogue in Christendom."

"And he also," asked the Colonel, "is a permanency—like yourself, if I may so without offense?"

"Indeed, he is a permanency in a very different sense from me," replied Mr. Malthus. "I have been graciously spared, but I must go at last. Now he never plays. He shuffles and deals for the club, and makes the necessary arrangements. That man, my dear Mr. Hammersmith, is the very soul of ingenuity. For three years he has pursued in London his useful and, I think I may add, his artistic calling; and not so much as a whisper of suspicion has been once aroused. I believe him myself to be inspired. You doubtless remember the celebrated case, six months ago, of the gentleman who was accidentally poisoned in a chemist's shop? That was one of

260

the least rich, one of the least racy, of his notions; but then, how simple! and how safe!"

"You astound me," said the Colonel. "Was that unfortunate gentleman one of the——" He was about to say "victims"; but bethinking himself in time, he substituted—"members of the club?"

In the same flash of thought, it occurred to him that Mr. Malthus himself had not at all spoken in the tone of one who is in love with death; and he added hurriedly:

"But I perceive I am still in the dark. You speak of shuffling and dealing; pray for what end? And since you seem rather unwilling to die than otherwise, I must own that I can not conceive what brings you here at all."

"You say truly that you are in the dark," replied Mr. Malthus with more animation. "Why, my dear sir, this club is the temple of intoxication. If my enfeebled health could support the excitement more often, you may depend upon it I should be more often here. It requires all the sense of duty engendered by a long habit of ill-health and careful regimen, to keep me from excess in this, which is, I may say, my last dissipation. I have tried them all, sir," he went on, laying his hand on Geraldine's arm, "all without exception, and I declare to you, upon my honor, there is not one of them that has not been grossly and untruthfully overrated. People trifle with love. Now, I deny that love is a strong passion.

Fear is the strong passion; it is with fear that you must trifle, if you wish to taste the intense joys of living. Envy me—envy me, sir," he added with a chuckle, "I am a coward!"

Geraldine could scarcely repress a movement of repulsion for this deplorable wretch; but he commanded himself with an effort, and continued his inquiries.

"How, sir," he asked, "is the excitement so artfully prolonged? and where is there any element of uncertainty?"

"I must tell you how the victim for every evening is selected," returned Mr. Malthus; "and not only the victim, but another member, who is to be the instrument in the club's hands, and death's high priest of that occasion."

"Good God!" said the Colonel, "do they then kill each other?"

"The trouble of suicide is removed in that way," returned Malthus with a nod.

"Merciful Heavens!" ejaculated the Colonel, "and may you—may I—may the—my friend, I mean—may any of us be pitched upon this evening as the slayer of another man's body and immortal spirit? Can such things be possible among men born of women? Oh, infamy of infamies!"

He was about to rise in his horror, when he caught the Prince's eye. It was fixed upon him from across the room with a frowning and angry stare. And in a moment Geraldine recovered his composure.

"After all," he added, "why not? And since you say the game is interesting, *vogue la galère* —I follow the club!"

Mr. Malthus had keenly enjoyed the Colonel's amazement and disgust. He had the vanity of wickedness; and it pleased him to see another man give way to a generous movement, while he felt himself, in his entire corruption, superior to such emotions.

"You now, after your first moment of surprise," said he, "are in a position to appreciate the delights of our society. You can see how it combines the excitement of a gaming-table, a duel, and a Roman amphitheater. The Pagans did well enough; I cordially admire the refinement of their minds; but it has been reserved for a Christian country to attain this extreme, this quintessence, this absolute of poignancy. You will understand how vapid are all amusements to a man who has acquired a taste for this one. The game we play," he continued, "is one of extreme simplicity. A full pack—but I perceive you are about to see the thing in progress. Will you lend me the help of your arm? I am unfortunately paralyzed."

Indeed, just as Mr. Malthus was beginning his description, another pair of folding-doors was thrown open, and the whole club began to pass, not without some hurry, into the adjoining room.

It was similar in every respect to the one from which it was entered, but somewhat differently furnished. The centre was occupied by a long green table, at which the President sat shuffling a pack of cards with great particularity. Even with the stick and the Colonel's arm, Mr. Malthus walked with so much difficulty that every one was seated before this pair and the Prince, who had waited for them, entered the apartment; and, in consequence, the three took seats close together at the lower end of the board.

"It is a pack of fifty-two," whispered Mr. Malthus. "Watch for the ace of spades, which is the sign of death, and the ace of clubs, which designates the official of the night. Happy, happy young men!" he added. "You have good eyes, and can follow the game. Alas! I can not tell an ace from a deuce across the table."

And he proceeded to equip himself with a second pair of spectacles.

"I must at least watch the faces," he explained.

The Colonel rapidly informed his friend of all that he had learned from the honorary member, and of the horrible alternative that lay before them. The Prince was conscious of a deadly chill and a contraction about his heart; he swallowed with difficulty, and looked from side to side like a man in a maze.

"One bold stroke," whispered the Colonel, "and we may still escape."

But the suggestion recalled the Prince's spirits.

"Silence!" said he. "Let me see that you can play like a gentleman for any stake, however serious."

And he looked about him, once more to all appearance at his ease, although his heart beat thickly, and he was conscious of an unpleasant heat in his bosom. The members were all very quiet and intent; every one was pale, but none so pale as Mr. Malthus. His eyes protruded; his head kept nodding involuntarily upon his spine; his hands found their way, one after the other, to his mouth, where they made clutches at his tremulous and ashen lips. It was plain that the honorary member enjoyed his membership on very startling terms.

"Attention, gentlemen!" said the President.

And he began slowly dealing the cards about the table in the reverse direction, pausing until each man had shown his card. Nearly every one hesitated; and sometimes you would see a player's fingers stumble more than once before he could turn over the momentous slip of pasteboard. As the Prince's turn drew nearer, he was conscious of a growing and almost suffocating excitement; but he had somewhat of the gambler's nature, and recognized almost with astonishment that there was a degree of pleasure in his sensations. The nine of clubs fell to his lot; the three of spades was dealt to Geraldine; and the queen of hearts to Mr. Malthus, who was unable to suppress a sob of relief. The young man of the cream tarts almost immediately afterward turned over the ace of clubs, and remained frozen with horror, the card still resting on his finger; he had not come there to kill, but to be killed; and the Prince, in his generous sympathy with his position, almost forgot the peril that still hung over himself and his friend.

The deal was coming round again, and still Death's card had not come out. The players held their respiration, and only breathed by gasps. The Prince received another club; Geraldine had a diamond; but when Mr. Malthus turned up his card a horrible noise, like that of something breaking, issued from his mouth; and he rose from his seat and sat down again, with no sign of his paralysis. It was the ace of spades. The honorary member had trifled once too often with his terrors.

Conversation broke out again almost at once. The players relaxed their rigid attitudes, and began to rise from the table and stroll back by twos and threes into the smoking-room. The President stretched his arms and yawned, like a man who had finished his day's work. But Mr. Malthus sat in his place, with his head in his hands, and his hands upon the table, drunk and motionless—a thing stricken down.

The Prince and Geraldine made their escape at once. In the cold night air their horror of what they had witnessed was redoubled.

"Alas!" cried the Prince, "to be bound by an

oath in such a matter! to allow this wholesale trade in murder to be continued with profit and impunity! If I but dared to forfeit my pledge!"

"That is impossible for your Highness," replied the Colonel, whose honor is the honor of Bohemia. "But I dare, and may with propriety, forfeit mine."

"Geraldine," said the Prince, "if your honor suffers in any of the adventures into which you follow me, not only will I never pardon you, but —what I believe will much more sensibly affect you—I should never forgive myself."

"I receive your Highness's commands," replied the Colonel. "Shall we go from this accursed spot?"

"Yes," said the Prince. "Call a cab in Heaven's name, and let me try to forget in slumber the memory of this night's disgrace."

But it was notable that he carefully read the name of the court before he left it.

The next morning, as soon as the Prince was stirring, Colonel Geraldine brought him a daily newspaper, with the following paragraph marked:

"MELANCHOLY ACCIDENT.—This morning, about two o'clock, Mr. Bartholomew Malthus, of 16 Chepstow Place, Westbourne Grove, on his way home from a party at a friend's house, fell over the upper parapet in Trafalgar Square, fracturing his skull and breaking a leg and an arm. Death was instantaneous. Mr. Malthus, accompanied by a friend, was engaged in looking for a cab at the time of the unfortunate occurrence. As Mr. Malthus was paralytic, it is thought that his fall may have been occasioned by another seizure. The unhappy gentleman was well known in the most respectable circles, and his loss will be widely and deeply deplored."

Florizel, "I always regret when you oblige me to remember my rank. Dispose of your day as you think fit, but be here before eleven in the same disguise."

The club, on this second evening, was not so fully attended; and when Geraldine and the Prince arrived, there were not above half a dozen persons in the smoking-room. His Highness took the President aside and congratulated him warmly on the demise of Mr. Malthus.

"I like," he said, "to meet with capacity, and certainly find much of it in you. Your profession is of a very delicate nature, but I see you are well qualified to conduct it with success and secrecy."

The President was somewhat affected by these compliments from one of his Highness's superior bearing. He acknowledged them almost with humility.

"Poor Malthy!" he added, "I shall hardly know the club without him. The most of my patrons are boys, sir, and poetical boys, who are not much company for me. Not but what Malthy had some poetry, too; but it was of a kind that I could understand."

"I can readily imagine you should find yourself in sympathy with Mr. Malthus," returned the Prince. "He struck me as a man of a very original disposition."

The young man of the cream tarts was in the room, but painfully depressed and silent. His late companions sought in vain to lead him into conversation.

"How bitterly I wish," he cried, "that I had never brought you to this infamous abode! Begone, while you are clean-handed. If you could have heard the old man scream as he fell, and the noise of his bones upon the pavement! Wish me, if you have any kindness to so fallen a being—wish the ace of spades for me, tonight!"

A few more members dropped in as the evening went on, but the club did not muster more than the devil's dozen when they took their places at the table. The Prince was again conscious of a certain joy in his alarms; but he was astonished to see Geraldine so much more self-possessed than on the night before.

"It is extraordinary," thought the Prince, "that a will, made or unmade, should so greatly influence a young man's spirit."

"Attention, gentlemen!" said the President, and he began to deal.

Three times the cards went all around the table, and neither of the marked cards had yet fallen from his hand. The excitement as he began the fourth distribution was overwhelming. There were just cards enough to go once more entirely round. The Prince, who sat second from the dealer's left, would receive, in the reverse mode of dealing practised at the club, the second last card. The third player picked up a black ace—it was the ace of clubs. The next received a diamond, the next a heart, and so on; but the ace of spades was still undelivered. At last Geraldine, who sat upon the Prince's left, turned his card; it was an ace, but the ace of hearts.

When Prince Florizel saw his fate upon the table in front of him, his heart stood still. He was a brave man, but the sweat poured off his face. There were exactly fifty chances out of a hundred that he was doomed. He reversed the card; it was the ace of spades. A loud roaring filled his brain, and the table swam before his eyes. He heard the player on his right break into a fit of laughter that sounded between mirth and disappointment; he saw the company rapidly dispersing, but his mind was full of other thoughts. He recognized how foolish, how criminal, had been his conduct. In perfect health, in the prime of his years, the heir to a throne, he had gambled away his future and that of a brave and loyal country. "God," he cried, "God forgive me!" And with that, the confusion of his senses passed away, and he regained his self-possession in a moment.

To his surprise Geraldine had disappeared. There was no one in the card-room but his destined butcher consulting with the President, and the young man of the cream tarts, who slipped up to the Prince and whispered in his ear:

"I would give a million, if I had it, for your luck."

His Highness could not help reflecting, as the young man departed, that he would have sold his opportunity for a much more moderate sum.

The whispered conference now came to an end. The holder of the ace of clubs left the room with a look of intelligence, and the President, approaching the unfortunate Prince, proffered him his hand.

"I am pleased to have met you, sir," said he, "and pleased to have been in a position to do you this trifling service. At least, you can not complain of delay. On the second evening—what a stroke of luck!"

The Prince endeavored in vain to articulate something in response, but his mouth was dry and his tongue seemed paralyzed.

"You feel a little sickish?" asked the President, with some show of solicitude. "Most gentlemen do. Will you take a little brandy?"

The Prince signified in the affirmative, and the other immediately poured some of the spirit into a tumbler.

"Poor old Malthy!" ejaculated the President, as the Prince drained the glass. "He drank near upon a pint, and little enough good it seemed to do him!"

"I am more amenable to treatment," said the Prince, a good deal revived. "I am my own man again at once, as you perceive. And so, let me ask you, what are my directions?"

"You will proceed along the Strand in the direction of the City, and on the left-hand pavement, until you meet the gentleman who has just left the room. He will continue your instructions, and him you will have the kindness to obey; the authority of the club is vested in his person for the night. And now," added the President, "I wish you a pleasant walk."

Florizel acknowledged the salutation rather awkwardly, and took his leave. He passed through the smoking-room, where the bulk of the players were still consuming champagne, some of which he had himself ordered and paid for; and he was surprised to find himself cursing them in his heart. He put on his hat and great-coat in the cabinet, and selected his umbrella from a corner. The familiarity of these acts, and the thought that he was about them for the last time, betrayed him into a fit of laughter which sounded unpleasantly in his own ears. He conceived a reluctance to leave the cabinet, and turned instead to the window. The sight of the lamps and the darkness recalled him to himself.

"Come, come, I must be a man," he thought, "and tear myself away."

At the corner of Box Court three men fell upon Prince Florizel and he was unceremoniously thrust into a carriage, which at once drove rapidly away. There was already an occupant.

"Will your Highness pardon my zeal?" said a well-known voice.

The Prince threw himself upon the Colonel's neck in a passion of relief.

"How can I ever thank you?" he cried. "And how was this effected?"

Although he had been willing to march upon his doom, he was overjoyed to yield to friendly violence, and return once more to life and hope.

"You can thank me effectually enough," replied the Colonel, "by avoiding all such dangers in the future. And as for your second question, all has been managed by the simplest means. I arranged this afternoon with a celebrated detective. Secrecy has been promised and paid for. Your own servants have been principally engaged in the affair. The house in Box Court has been surrounded since nightfall, and this, which is one of your own carriages, has been awaiting you for nearly an hour."

"And the miserable creature who was to have slain me—what of him?" inquired the Prince.

"He was pinioned as he left the club," replied the Colonel, "and now awaits your sentence at the Palace, where he will soon be joined by his accomplices."

"Geraldine," said the Prince, "you have saved me against my explicit orders, and you have done well. I owe you not only my life, but a lesson; and I should be unworthy of my rank if I did not show myself grateful to my teacher. Let it be yours to choose the manner."

forth upon his travels, under the supervision of
Mr. Geraldine, and a pair of faithful and adroit
lackeys, well trained in the Prince's household.
Not content with this, discreet agents were put in
possession of the house of Box Court, and all
letters of visitors for the Suicide Club or its
officials were to be examined by Prince Florizel
in person.

THE FOUNTAIN OF YOUTH

BY RUDOLF BAUMBACH

THE FOUNTAIN OF YOUTH

BY RUDOLF BAUMBACH

IT was on the day of the summer solstice, and the glow of midday lay on the corn-fields. At times a fresh wind swept over from the mountain forest near; then the stalks bent low, and the poppies on the edge of the field scattered their delicate petals. Crickets and grasshoppers chirped in the grain, and from the blackthorn on the roadside the goldhammer once in a while let her gentle call be heard.

Through the corn-field, which extended from the valley to the mountain, walked, in the narrow path, a young woman of slender yet strong figure. She wore the customary plaited skirt, and, for protection against the sun's rays, a red kerchief; on her left arm hung a basket, and in her right hand she carried a stone jug.

As the goldhammer in the thorn-hedge became aware of her presence he fluttered to the highest twig and called softly: "Maiden, maiden, how do you flourish?" But the bird was mistaken. The blond Greta was no maiden, but a young wife, and now was on her way to her husband, who felled wood in the forest above.

Translated by Minnie B. Hudson. Copyright, 1891, by The Current Literature Publishing Company.

When the fair one had reached the border of the forest she stood listening, and soon the strokes of a woodman's ax told her where to turn her steps. It was not long before she saw her husband, who felled a pine tree with mighty strokes, and, with joyful voice, she called to him.

"Remain standing where thou art," responded he. "The tree will fall directly." And the pine tree gave a deep sigh, bowed itself, and sank crashing to the earth.

Now Greta came nearer, and the sunburnt woodcutter took his young wife in his arms and kissed her fondly. Then she sat down on the trunk of the tree, and took the food from the basket she had brought. Here Hans laid down the bread from his hand, took his ax, and said: "I have forgotten something," stepped in the direction of the fallen pine, and cut three crosses in the wood.

"Why dost thou that, Hans?" asked the wife.

"That was done on account of the woodsprites," explained the husband. "The poor creatures have a wicked enemy, who is the wild hunter. Day and night he waylays them and hunts them with his dogs. But if the pursued little women succeed in escaping to such a tree-trunk, then the wild huntsman can not harm them, because of the three crosses."

The young wife's eyes grew large. "Hast thou ever met a wood-sprite?" asked she, curious.

"No. They only rarely let themselves be seen.

But to-day is the solstice, when they become visible." And suddenly he called with a loud voice into the forest: "Wood-sprite, appear!"

He had only done this in order to tease his wife; but, on the holy midsummer day, one should not jest about such things.

At once a little woman, a yard high, delicate of form and very beautiful of face, stood before the pair. She wore a long white garment, and in her golden hair a spray of mistletoe.

Hans and Greta were very much frightened. They rose up hastily from their seats, and Greta made a bow, the best she could do.

"You have called me at a good time," said the wood-sprite, and pointed with forefinger to the orb of the sun, that stood almost over her head, "and a good deed"—here the little woman pointed to the marked tree-stump—"is the other reason. Gold and silver have I not to give away, but I know something better. Come with me; it will do you no harm, and take your jug: you will be able to make use of it."

So she spoke and led the way. Hans shouldered his woodman's ax, Greta took up the stone jug, and both followed the little woman. She had a walk like a duck, and Greta plucked her husband's sleeve, pointed to the waddling little woman, and would have whispered something into his ear, but Hans laid his forefinger on her mouth. Nothing hurts a sprite more than to have a person ridicule their gait. They have feet like

every Sunday, when the church-bell rang, each drank a drop from the flask.

Then once again the day of the summer solstice drew near. On the evening before, Hans and Greta sat before their door and looked toward the heights where the St. John's fire blazed, and from the distance sounded the mirth of the young fellows and maids, who stirred the fire and sprang through its flames in couples.

Then the wife said: "Dear Hans, I would like to go once more to the forest. If thou desirest it also, then will we start early in the morning. But thou must waken me early, for when the elder blossoms the young women like to sleep until the sun is high in the heavens."

Hans agreed. On the next morning he wakened his wife, and they went together into the forest. They walked like lovers, and each gave a careful heed to the steps of the other.

When Hans cautiously jumped over the root of a tree, the wife said: "Ah, Hans, thou leapest indeed like a young kid!" and when Greta timidly stepped over a little ditch, her husband laughed and cried: "Tuck up your dress, Greta! Jump!" And then they selected an old pine tree, feasting in its shade on what Greta had brought with her.

"It was here," said Hans, "where the wood-sprite appeared to us that day, and there yonder must lie the forest meadow with the fountain of youth. But I have never again found the meadow and the spring."

THE FOUNTAIN OF YOUTH

"And, God be thanked! that has mattered not," hastily interrupted Greta. "For our flask is still far from being empty."

"Certainly, certainly," nodded Hans. "But yet it would please me if we could see the wood-sprite once again, and thank her for our good fortune. Come—let us go and seek her. Perhaps I will be as lucky to-day as formerly."

Then they set out and went deeper into the forest, and after a quarter of an hour saw there before their eyes, the sunny forest meadow. Lilies and bluebells bloomed in the grass, gay-colored butterflies flew to and fro, and on the edge of the forest stood also the little house, just as in years before. They went toward the house with beating hearts, and best of all, there was indeed the fountain of youth at hand, and dragon-flies, in green and gold, hovered over it.

Hans and Greta stepped to the brim of the spring. They embraced each other and stooped over the water; and from out the clear surface of the spring there confronted them two gray heads with friendly, wrinkled faces.

Then hot tears fell from the eyes of the old couple, and they stood stammering and sobbing in mutual guilt. It required a long time before it became clear to them that each had deluded and for long years had lovingly deceived the other.

"Thou hast also known that we have both grown old?" cried out Hans, joyfully.

"Of course, of course," laughed the wife, amid tears.

"And I, also," rejoiced old Hans. Then he took his wife and kissed her as on the day she had said "Yes" to him.

Then the forest-sprite suddenly stood before them, as if she had sprung out of the earth.

"Welcome," said she. "You have not appeared before me for a long time. But—but," continued the little woman, and threatened with her finger, "you have kept a bad home with the water of youth. Wrinkles and gray hair! Ah, ah! Now," continued she again, "that is easy to remedy, and you are come at a good hour. Quick! Spring into the fountain of youth; it is not deep; dip your gray heads under; then you shall see a miracle. The bath will restore to you youthful vigor and beauty. But quick, before the sun sinks!"

Hans and Greta looked at each other.

"Wilt thou?" asked the husband, in an uncertain voice.

"Never," answered Greta, quickly. "Oh, if thou only knowest how happy I am, that at last I may be old! And, also, it would be impossible on account of our children and grandchildren. No, gracious forest-sprite, a thousand thanks for your good deed, but we remain as we are. Is it not so, Hans?"

"Yes," nodded Hans, "we remain old. If thou

couldst but know, Greta, how well your gray hair becomes you."

"As you will," said the wood-sprite, a little vexed. "There is no ceremony here." So speaking, she went into the house and locked the door behind her.

But the old couple kissed each other anew. Then they stepped homeward, arm in arm, through the forest, and the midsummer sun shed a golden light upon their gray heads.

BOLESS

BY MAXIM GORKI

BOLESS

BY MAXIM GORKI

A N ACQUAINTANCE of mine once told me the following story:

"While still a student at Moscow I happened to be living alongside one of those—well, she was a Polish woman, Teresa by name. A tall, powerfully built brunette with heavy, bushy eyebrows, and a large, coarse, vulgar face, as if carved out with an ax—the animal gleam of her eyes, the deep bass voice, the gait and manners of a cabman, and her immense strength like that of a market-woman, inspired me with an inexpressible horror. I lived in the garret of the house, and her room was opposite mine. I never opened my door when I knew that she was in. But this, of course, happened very rarely. Sometimes I chanced to meet her on the landing, staircase, or in the yard, and she would look at me with a smile which seemed to me cynical and rapacious. Occasionally I saw her in her cups, with bleary eyes, her hair and clothes in disorder and with a particularly loathsome smile. On such occasions she would meet my eye with an impudent stare and say:

" 'How are you, Pan Student?' [1]

"And her stupid laugh would increase my dislike for her still more. I would have liked nothing better than to change my quarters in order to get rid of her proximity, but my room was so nice, and the view from my window was so fine, the street below so quiet and peaceful, that I concluded to endure it.

"One morning after I had dressed and was sprawling on the cot, trying to invent some sort of an excuse for not attending my classes, the door of my room suddenly opened, and the disgusting bass voice of the Polish woman sounded from the threshold:

" 'Good morning, Pan Student!'

" 'What is it you wish?' I asked her. I saw she looked confused and had in her face a kind of pleading expression, something unusual with her.

" 'You see, Pan Student, I came to beg you to do me a great favor. Don't refuse me, please!'

"Lying there on my cot I thought that it was just some pretext or other to make my further acquaintance. Take care, my boy!

" 'You see, I have to send a letter to my native country,' she continued in a supplicating, low, tremulous voice.

" 'Well,' I thought, 'the devil take you. If you wish I will write it for you.' And springing to my feet I sat down to the table, took some paper

[1] Pan is Polish for Mister.

and said: 'Well, come nearer; sit down and dictate.'

"She came over; sat down cautiously on the edge of the chair and looked at me in rather a guilty way.

" 'To whom shall I write?'

" 'To Boleslav Kapshat, in the town Sventsiani, on the Warsaw railroad.'

" 'Well, what shall I write? Speak.'

" 'My dearest Boless, my heart's delight, my beloved. May the Mother of God protect you! My golden heart, why have you not written for so long a time to your sorrowing dove, Teresa—'

"I could hardly keep from laughing. A sorrowing dove, indeed! Almost six feet tall, with the fists of a prize-fighter, and a face so black that it seemed as if the 'dove' had been sweeping chimneys all her life and had never thoroughly washed herself. But I somehow kept my face straight and asked:

" 'Who is this Bolesst?'

" 'Boless, Pan Student,' she replied seemingly offended because of my mispronouncing the name. 'He is my affianced.'

" 'Affianced!'

" 'And why are you so astonished? Can not I, a girl, have an affianced?'

"She—a girl! well, this beats everything I ever heard. Oh, well, who can tell about such matters! Everything is possible in this world.

" 'And have you been long engaged?'

" 'The sixth year.'

" 'Oh, oh!' I thought and then said aloud: 'Well, go ahead with your letter.'

"And I must confess—so tender and loving was this message—that I would have willingly exchanged places with this Boless had the fair correspondent been any one else but Teresa.

" 'I thank you from my inmost soul for your favor, Pan Student,' Teresa said, bowing low. 'Can I in any way be of service to you?'

" 'No, thank you.'

" 'But maybe the Pan's shirts or trousers need mending?'

"This made me quite angry. I felt that this mastodon in petticoats was making the blood mount to my cheeks, and I told her quite sharply that her services were not required; and she departed.

"Two weeks or so passed. One evening I was sitting at my window, softly whistling and thinking hard how to get away from myself. I felt very bored. The weather was as nasty as it could be. To go out that evening was out of the question, and having nothing better to do I began from sheer ennui a course of self-analysis. This proved dull enough work, but there was nothing else to do. Suddenly the door opened, thank God! Some one was coming to see me.

" 'Are you very busy just now, Pan Student?'

" 'Teresa! H'm—' I thought I would have

preferred any one at all to her. Then I said aloud.

" 'No, what is it you want now?'

" 'I wish to ask the Pan Student to write me another letter.'

"Very well. Is it again to Boless you wish me to write?'

" 'No, this time I want you to write a letter from Boless to me.'

" 'Wha-at?'

" 'I beg your pardon, Pan Student. How stupid of me! It is not for me, this letter, but for a friend of mine, a man acquaintance; he has a fiancée. Her name is like mine, Teresa. He does not know how to write, so I want the Pan Student to write for him a letter to that Teresa—'

"I looked at her. She seemed very confused and frightened, and her fingers trembled. And though I failed at first to understand what was the matter with her I at last understood.

" 'Look here, my lady,' I said to her. 'You have been telling me a pack of lies. There are no Bolesses nor Teresas among your acquaintances. It is only a pretext for coming in here. I tell you outright that there is no use of coming sneaking around me, as I do not wish to have anything to do with you. Do you understand?'

"She grew very red in the face and I saw that she was strangely frightened and confused, and

301

moved her lips so oddly, wishing to say something, without being able to say it. And somehow I began to think that I had misjudged her a little. There was somehing behind all this. But what?

" 'Pan Student,' she suddenly began, but broke off, and turning toward the door walked out of the room.

"I remained with a very unpleasant feeling in my heart. I heard her shut her own door with a bang; evidently the poor girl was very angry—I thought the matter over and decided to go in to her and induce her to return; I would write her the letter she wished.

"I entered her room. She was sitting at the table with her head pressed in her hands.

" 'Teresa,' I said, 'will you listen to me a moment?'

"Whenever I come to this turn of the story I always feel very awkward and embarrassed. But let us return to my narrative. Seeing that she did not reply I repeated:

" 'Listen to me, my girl—'

"She sprang to her feet, came close up to me, with eyes flashing, and placing her two hands on my shoulders she began to whisper, or rather to hum in her deep bass voice:

" 'Look you here, Pan Student. What of it, what of it if there is no Boless? And what if there is no Teresa? What difference does it make to you? Is it so hard for you to draw a few lines on the paper! Oh, you! And I thought you such a good fellow, such a nice fair-haired little boy. Yes, it is true—there is no Boless, and there is no Teresa, there is only me! Well, what of it?'

" 'Allow me,' I said greatly disconcerted by this reception. 'What is it you are saying? Is there no Boless?'

" 'Yes, there is none. But what of it?'

" 'And no Teresa either?'

" 'No, no Teresa either; that is, yes, I am her.'

"I could not understand a word. I stared straight into her eyes, trying to determine which of us two had lost our reason. And she returned once more to the table, rummaged for some time in the drawer, and coming back to me said in an offended tone:

" 'Here is the letter you wrote for me, take it back. You do not wish to write me a second one anyway. Others will probably be kinder than you and would do so.'

"I recognized the letter she held out to me as the one I wrote for her to Boless. Humph!

" 'Look here, Teresa,' I said to her. 'Will you please explain to me what it all means? Why do you ask people to write letters for you when you do not find it necessary even to post them?'

" 'Post them? Where to?'

" 'Why, to this Boless, of course.'

" 'But he does not exist!'

"I really could not understand a word. There

303

was nothing left for me to do but to spit and walk out of the room. But she explained herself.

" 'Well, what of it?' she began in an offended voice. 'He does not exist. He does not, so,' and she extended her hands as if she could not herself clearly understand why he did not exist in reality. 'But I want him to. Am I not as much of a human being as the others? Of course I—I know— But it does no harm to any one, that I am writing to him—'

" 'Allow me—to whom?'

" 'To Boless, of course.'

" 'But he does not exist.'

" 'Oh, Mother of God! What if he does not exist? He does not; still to me he does. And Teresa—this is myself, and he replies to my letters, and I write to him again.'

"I understood. I felt so sick at heart, so ashamed of myself to know that alongside of me, only three paces removed, lived a human being who had no one in the whole world to love and sympathize with her, and that this being had to invent a friend for herself.

" 'Here you have written a letter from me to Boless, and I gave it to another to read, and when I hear it read it really begins to seem to me as if there is a Boless. And then I ask that a letter be written from Boless to Teresa—that is to me. And when such a letter is written and is read to me then I am almost entirely convinced that there is a Boless, and that makes my life easier.'

"Yes, the devil take it all," continued my acquaintance. "To make a long story short I began from that time on to write with the greatest punctuality twice a week letters to Boless and vice versa. I wrote splendid replies to her. She used to listen to my reading of those epistles and to weep in her bass voice. In return for this she used to mend my clothes and darn my socks.

"Three months later she was thrown into prison for some reason or other and by now she must surely be dead."

My acquaintance blew the ashes from his cigarette, looked thoughtfully at the sky, and concluded:

"Y-e-s, the more a human being has drunk of the cup of bitterness the more ardently he longs for sweetness. And we, enveloped in our worn-out virtues and gazing at each other through the haze of self-sufficiency and convinced of our righteousness, fail to understand it.

"And the whole affair turns out very stupid, and very cruel. Fallen people we say—but who and what are those fallen ones? First of all they are human beings of the very same bone and blood, of the very same flesh and nerves as ourselves. We have been told the very same thing for whole ages, day in and day out. And we listen and—and the devil alone knows how stupid it all is! In reality we, too, are but fallen people and more deeply fallen too, probably—into the abyss of self-sufficiency, convinced of our own sinlessness and superiority, the superiority of our own nerves and brains over the nerves and brains of those who are only less crafty than we are, and who can not, as we can, feign a goodness they do not possess—but enough of this. It is all so old and stale—so old and stale indeed that one is ashamed to speak of it—"

THE SILVER CRUCIFIX

BY ANTONIO FOGAZZARO

manded the Countess. "Have you seen your master yet? Why, you are trembling all over! What is the matter with you?"

What, indeed, ailed the girl? Cup, saucer, sugar-bowl, and coffee-pot were rattling on the tray. "What is it?" repeated the Countess.

If the maid's face showed signs of alarm, no less was the mistress disturbed by doubts and fears.

"Nothing," replied the servant, still trembling.

The Countess hereupon seized her by the arm, shook it roughly, and exclaimed:

"Tell me!"

Meanwhile the pretty little head of a child of four was peering over the edge of the crib.

"It's a case," said the maid, half in tears, "it's a case of cholera."

Pale as death, the lady started up, and instinctively looked at her listening son. She jumped out of bed; by a single gesture she imposed silence on the girl, while motioning her to go into the next room. Then she darted to her child's crib.

The little fellow had begun to cry again, but his mother kissed and petted him, played and laughed with him until he forgot his woes, and stopped weeping. She pulled on her dressing-gown in great haste, and joined the servant, shutting the door behind her.

"Oh, my God, my God!" lamented the girl between her sobs, while the other woman too began to shed tears.

"Hush, for Heaven's sake! On no account must baby be frightened! What about this case —where is it?"

"Here, milady! Rosa, the steward's wife. She was taken ill at midnight."

"Heavens! And now—?"

"She is dead. She died half an hour ago."

The baby was shrilly clamoring for his mother.

"Go," said the Countess; "go in and play with him. Keep him happy; do anything you like. Be quiet, darling!" she exclaimed. "I shall be back in a moment." Upon which she rushed to the Count's room.

The lady was blindly, insanely afraid of the cholera; nothing but her passion for her child could have been more intense than this feeling. At the first rumors of the epidemic she and her husband had fled the city, escaping to their splendid country seat—her marriage portion—in the hope that the disease would not spread thither. The place had been spared in 1836, and had even remained untouched in 1886. And now there it was, in the farmyard attached to the villa.

Disheveled and untidy, she flew into her husband's room. Before speaking she gave two violent tugs at the bellrope.

"Have you heard?" she said, with flaming eyes. The Count, who was phlegmatically shaving his beard, turned round, inquiring, with the soapy brush in his hand: "What?"

"Don't you know about Rosa?"

"Oh, yes, I know," was his calm response.

If, in the first place, the Count had cherished some vague illusion that his wife was ignorant of Rosa's death, it now also seemed proper to re-assure her by his cool demeanor. Instead, however, her ladyship's eyes shot fire, and her features were savage with anger.

"What!" she shouted, "you know, and you can think of nothing better to do than shave? What sort of man are you—what sort of father—what sort of husband?"

"Good Lord!" cried the Count, throwing up his arms.

But before the poor man, soaped up to the eyes, and wrapped round with a towel, could add another word, in came the valet. Her ladyship commanded that not a peasant from the farm-yard should be admitted to the house, and that no one should go thence to the farmyard. After this she gave orders for the coachman to be ready within an hour; he must harness to the landau the horses which his lordship would select.

"What are you going to do?" asked the latter, who had recovered himself meanwhile. "Nothing rash, I must insist."

"*Rash*—how dare you say that? I am willing to be obedient to you in everything, but when it comes to a question of life and death—my son's

life, you understand—then I will listen to no
parley from any one. I wish to leave here at
once. Order the horses, please."

The Count grew annoyed. How could matters
have come to such a pass as this? Was there any
propriety in running away after such a fashion?
And then, what about business affairs? In two
days, or one day, or maybe in twelve hours, he
would be ready to start. But not before—no.
His wife, however, interrupted him violently:
"Propriety, indeed, and business! For shame!"

"And clothes?" objected the husband. "We
must certainly take some with us. You see, we
shall really need more time."

The Countess made some contemptuous answer. She would see to it, she assured him, that
the trunks were packed in an hour.

"But where do you expect to go?" persisted the
Count.

"To the railway station, first of all, and then
wherever you like. Now order the horses."

"I have had enough of this!" cried the other.
"I'll give such orders as I choose! I'll let the
business affairs go, and everything else! Your
clothes, too! The sorrels," he added, enraged, to
the domestic who was standing by impassively.

The Countess dressed and did her hair with
the utmost speed, at moments clasping her hands
in silent prayer, distributing commands, sum-
moning servants from various parts of the house
by frantic pulls at the bell. There was running

not soaked by the rain dripping from the roof.

Crouching on the floor, head leaning against the edge of the bed, sat the peasant's cholera-stricken wife. Although but thirty, she looked old; at twenty she had been a blooming girl, and even now preserved remnants of mild beauty. At a glance her husband understood; he swallowed an imprecation. The child, frightened by his mother's discolored face, kept in the doorway.

"For Christ's sake, send him away," she moaned feebly. "I have the cholera; send him away. Go to your aunt's, dear. Take him away, and send me the priest."

"I'll go," said the man to her; and to the boy, motioning toward the gate, "Go to your aunt's."

From the porch of the yard he fetched an armful of straw, carried it into the kitchen, and went upstairs to his wife, who by exerting all her strength had contrived to get on the bed.

"Listen," said the man, with unusual tenderness; "I am sorry, but if you die in the bed it will have to be burnt. You understand, don't you? I brought some straw into the kitchen—a nice lot."

Too weak to answer, she made a mute signal of assent, and then a faint effort to rise from her couch. But the man took her up in his arms. By a gesture she begged him to reach first for a small silver crucifix hanging on the wall; she pressed it fervidly to her lips while her husband carried her down to the kitchen. Here he made her as comfortable as he could on the straw, before going for the priest.

And now, this poor creature lying alone like a beast in a cage on the infected straw—she, too, before departing to an unknown world, began to pray. She prayed for the salvation of her soul, convinced she was guilty of many sins, and tormented by her inability to remember them.

When the timid doctor, sent by the mayor, arrived, he asked in great fright whether there was any rum or marsala in the house. There was neither—so he recommended hot bricks for her stomach, put up a notice of quarantine, and left her. The priest, who knew no fear, carelessly reeled off what he termed "the usual things," obscuring the divine message with words of his own. Nevertheless, though ignorant, the dying woman derived comfort and serenity.

His task done, the priest went. Meanwhile the husband had put a few more handfuls of straw under her back, and lit the fire to heat the bricks. His wife went on praying—less for her child than for the man whom she had pardoned so often, and who was embarked on the road to perdition. Finally, kissing the cross, her mind turned to its giver. She had received it sixteen years back, at her confirmation, from the Countess, the mistress of the splendid manor where it was a joy to live and of the wretched hovel where it was a joy to die. The Countess was then a young girl, and had given the silver crucifix to the laborer's daughter at the suggestion of her mother, then

THE MUMMY'S FOOT

BY THÉOPHILE GAUTIER

I HAD entered, in an idle mood, the shop of one of those curiosity-venders, who are called *marchands de bric-à-brac* in that Parisian *argot* which is so perfectly unintelligible elsewhere in France.

You have doubtless glanced occasionally through the windows of some of these shops, which have become so numerous now that it is fashionable to buy antiquated furniture, and that every petty stockbroker thinks he must have his *chambre au moyen âge*.

There is one thing there which clings alike to the shop of the dealer in old iron, the wareroom of the tapestry-maker, the laboratory of the chemist, and the studio of the painter—in all those gloomy dens where a furtive daylight filters in through the window-shutters the most manifestly ancient thing is dust;—the cobwebs are more authentic than the guimp laces; and the old pear-tree furniture on exhibition is actually younger than the mahogany which arrived but yesterday from America.

The warehouse of my bric-à-brac dealer was a veritable Capharnaum; all ages and all nations

Translated by Lafcadio Hearn.

seemed to have made their rendezvous there; an Etruscan lamp of red clay stood upon a Boule cabinet, with ebony panels, brightly striped by lines of inlaid brass; a duchess of the court of Louis XV nonchalantly extended her fawn-like feet under a massive table of the time of Louis XIII, with heavy spiral supports of oak, and carven designs of Chimeras and foliage intermingled.

Upon the denticulated shelves of several sideboards glittered immense Japanese dishes with red and blue designs relieved by gilded hatching; side by side with enameled works by Bernard Palissy, representing serpents, frogs, and lizards in relief.

From disemboweled cabinets escaped cascades of silver-lustrous Chinese silks and waves of tinsel, which an oblique sunbeam shot through with luminous beads; while portraits of every era, in frames more or less tarnished, smiled through their yellow varnish.

The striped breastplate of a damascened suit of Milanese armor glittered in one corner; Loves and Nymphs of porcelain; Chinese grotesques, vases of *céladon* and crackle-ware; Saxon and old Sèvres cups encumbered the shelves and nooks of the department.

The dealer followed me closely through the tortuous way contrived between the piles of furniture; warding off with his hand the hazardous sweep of my coat-skirts; watching my elbows

with the uneasy attention of an antiquarian and
a usurer.

It was a singular face, that of the merchant—
an immense skull, polished like a knee, and surrounded by a thin aureole of white hair, which
brought out the clear salmon tint of his complexion all the more strikingly, lent him a false aspect
of patriarchal *bonhomie,* counteracted, however,
by the scintillation of two little yellow eyes which
trembled in their orbits like two louis-d'or upon
quicksilver. The curve of his nose presented an
aquiline silhouette, which suggested the Oriental
or Jewish type. His hands—thin, slender, full
of nerves which projected like strings upon the
finger-board of a violin, and armed with claws
like those on the terminations of bats' wings—
shook with senile trembling; but those convulsively agitated hands became firmer than steel
pincers or lobsters' claws when they lifted any
precious article—an onyx cup, a Venetian glass,
or a dish of Bohemian crystal. This strange old
man had an aspect so thoroughly rabbinical and
cabalistic that he would have been burnt on the
mere testimony of his face three centuries ago.

"Will you not buy something from me to-day,
sir? Here is a Malay kreese with a blade undu-
lating like flame: look at those grooves contrived
for the blood to run along, those teeth set back-
ward so as to tear out the entrails in withdrawing
the weapon—it is a fine character of ferocious
arm, and will look well in your collection: this

two-handed sword is very beautiful—it is the
work of Josepe de la Hera; and this *coliche-
marde,* with its fenestrated guard—what a superb specimen of handicraft!"

"No; I have quite enough weapons and instru-
ments of carnage;—I want a small figure, something which will suit me as a paper-weight; for
I can not endure those trumpery bronzes which
the stationers sell, and which may be found on
everybody's desk."

The old gnome foraged among his ancient
wares, and finally arranged before me some antique bronzes—so-called, at least; fragments of
malachite; little Hindu or Chinese idols—a kind
of poussah-toys in jade-stone, representing the
incarnations of Brahma or Vishnu, and wonderfully appropriate to the very undivine office of
holding papers and letters in place.

I was hesitating between a porcelain dragon,
all constellated with warts—its mouth formidable
with bristling tusks and ranges of teeth—and an
abominable little Mexican fetish, representing
the god Vitziliputzili *au naturel;* when I caught
sight of a charming foot, which I at first took for
a fragment of some antique Venus.

It had those beautiful ruddy and tawny tints
that lend to Florentine bronze that warm, living
look so much preferable to the gray-green aspect
of common bronzes, which might easily be mistaken for statues in a state of putrefaction: satiny
gleams played over its rounded forms, doubtless

polished by the amorous kisses of twenty centuries; for it seemed a Corinthian bronze, a work of the best era of art—perhaps molded by Lysippus himself.

"That foot will be my choice," I said to the merchant, who regarded me with an ironical and saturnine air, and held out the object desired that I might examine it more fully.

I was surprised at its lightness; it was not a foot of metal, but in sooth a foot of flesh—an embalmed foot—a mummy's foot: on examining it still more closely the very grain of the skin, and the almost imperceptible lines impressed upon it by the texture of the bandages, became perceptible. The toes were slender and delicate, and terminated by perfectly formed nails, pure and transparent as agates; the great toe, slightly separated from the rest, afforded a happy contrast, in the antique style, to the position of the other toes, and lent it an aerial lightness—the grace of a bird's foot;—the sole, scarcely streaked by a few almost imperceptible cross lines, afforded evidence that it had never touched the bare ground, and had only come in contact with the finest matting of Nile rushes, and the softest carpets of panther skin.

"Ha, ha!—you want the foot of the Princess Hermonthis"—exclaimed the merchant, with a strange giggle, fixing his owlish eyes upon me—"ha, ha, ha!—for a paper-weight!—an original idea!—artistic idea! Old Pharaoh would cer-

out with the gravity and pride becoming one who feels that he has the ineffable advantage over all the passers-by whom he elbows, of possessing a piece of the Princess Hermonthis, daughter of Pharaoh.

I looked upon all who did not possess, like myself, a paper-weight so authentically Egyptian, as very ridiculous people; and it seemed to me that the proper occupation of every sensible man should consist in the mere fact of having a mummy's foot upon his desk.

Happily I met some friends, whose presence distracted me in my infatuation with this new acquisition: I went to dinner with them; for I could not very well have dined with myself.

When I came back that evening, with my brain slightly confused by a few glasses of wine, a vague whiff of Oriental perfume delicately titillated my olfactory nerves: the heat of the room had warmed the natron, bitumen, and myrrh in which the *paraschistes,* who cut open the bodies of the dead, had bathed the corpse of the princess;—it was a perfume at once sweet and penetrating—a perfume that four thousand years had not been able to dissipate.

The Dream of Egypt was Eternity: her odors have the solidity of granite, and endure as long.

I soon drank deeply from the black cup of sleep: for a few hours all remained opaque to me; Oblivion and Nothingness inundated me with their sombre waves.

THE MUMMY'S FOOT

Yet light gradually dawned upon the darkness of my mind: dreams commenced to touch me softly in their silent flight.

The eyes of my soul were opened; and I beheld my chamber as it actually was: I might have believed myself awake, but for a vague consciousness which assured me that I slept, and that something fantastic was about to take place.

The odor of the myrrh had augmented in intensity: and I felt a slight headache, which I very naturally attributed to several glasses of champagne that we had drunk to the unknown gods and our future fortunes.

I peered through my room with a feeling of expectation which I saw nothing to justify: every article of furniture was in its proper place; the lamp, softly shaded by its globe of ground crystal, burned upon its bracket; the water-color sketches shone under their Bohemian glass; the curtains hung down languidly; everything wore an aspect of tranquil slumber.

After a few moments, however, all this calm interior appeared to become disturbed; the woodwork cracked stealthily; the ash-covered log suddenly emitted a jet of blue flame; and the disks of the pateras seemed like great metallic eyes, watching, like myself, for the things which were about to happen.

My eyes accidentally fell upon the desk where I had placed the foot of the Princess Hermonthis.

apparition had but one foot; the other was broken off at the ankle!

She approached the table where the foot was starting and fidgeting about more than ever; and there supported herself upon the edge of the desk. I saw her eyes fill with pearly-gleaming tears.

Although she had not as yet spoken, I fully comprehended the thoughts which agitated her: she looked at her foot—for it was indeed her own —with an exquisitely graceful expression of co-quettish sadness; but the foot leaped and ran hither and thither, as though impelled on steel springs.

Twice or thrice she extended her hand to seize it, but could not succeed.

Then commenced between the Princess Her-monthis and her foot—which appeared to be en-dowed with a special life of its own—a very fan-tastic dialogue in a most ancient Coptic tongue, such as might have been spoken thirty centuries ago in the syrinxes of the land of Ser: luckily I understood Coptic perfectly well that night.

The Princess Hermonthis cried, in a voice sweet and vibrant as the tones of a crystal bell:

"Well, my dear little foot, you always flee from me; yet I always took good care of you. I bathed you with perfumed water in a bowl of alabaster; I smoothed your heel with pumice-stone mixed with palm oil; your nails were cut with golden scissors and polished with a hippopotamus tooth; I was careful to select *tatbebs* for you, painted and embroidered and turned up at the toes, which were the envy of all the young girls in Egypt: you wore on your great toe rings bearing the device of the sacred Scarabæus; and you supported one of the lightest bodies that a lazy foot could sustain.

The foot replied in a pouting and chagrined tone:

"You know well that I do not belong to myself any longer. I have been bought and paid for: the old merchant knew what he was about: he bore you a grudge for having refused to espouse him. This is an ill turn which he has done you. The Arab who violated your royal coffin in the subterranean pits of the necropolis of Thebes was sent thither by him: he desired to prevent you from being present at the reunion of the shadowy nations in the cities below. Have you five pieces of gold for my ransom?"

"Alas, no!—my jewels, my rings, my purses of gold and silver, were all stolen from me," answered the Princess Hermonthis, with a sob.

"Princess," I then exclaimed, "I never retained anybody's foot unjustly;—even though you have not got the five louis which it cost me, I present it to you gladly: I should feel unutterably wretched to think that I were the cause of so amiable a person as the Princess Hermonthis being lame."

I delivered this discourse in a royally gallant,

troubadour tone which must have astonished the beautiful Egyptian girl.

She turned a look of deepest gratitude upon me; and her eyes shone with bluish gleams of light.

She took her foot—which surrendered itself willingly this time—like a woman about to put on her little shoe; and adjusted it to her leg with much skill.

This operation over, she took a few steps about the room, as though to assure herself that she was really no longer lame.

"Ah, how pleased my father will be!—he who was so unhappy because of my mutilation; and who from the moment of my birth, set a whole nation at work to hollow me out a tomb so deep that he might preserve me intact until that last day, when souls must be weighed in the balance of Amenthi! Come with me to my father!—he will receive you kindly; for you have given me back my foot."

I thought this proposition natural enough. I arrayed myself in a dressing-gown of large-flowered pattern, which lent me a very Pharaonic aspect; hurriedly put on a pair of Turkish slippers, and informed the Princess Hermonthis that I was ready to follow her.

Before starting, Hermonthis took from her neck the little idol of green paste, and laid it on the scattered sheets of paper which covered the table.

"It is only fair," she observed, smilingly, "that I should replace your paper-weight."

She gave me her hand, which felt soft and cold, like the skin of a serpent; and we departed.

We passed for some time with the velocity of an arrow through a fluid and grayish expanse, in which half-formed silhouettes flitted swiftly by us, to right and left.

For an instant we saw only sky and sea.

A few moments later obelisks commenced to tower in the distance: pylons and vast flights of steps guarded by sphinxes became clearly outlined against the horizon.

We had reached our destination.

The princess conducted me to a mountain of rose-colored granite, in the face of which appeared an opening so narrow and low that it would have been difficult to distinguish it from the fissures in the rock, had not its location been marked by two stelæ wrought with sculptures.

Hermonthis kindled a torch, and led the way before me.

We traversed corridors hewn through the living rock: their walls, covered with hieroglyphics and paintings of allegorical processions, might well have occupied thousands of arms for thousands of years in their formation;—these corridors, of interminable length, opened into square chambers, in the midst of which pits had been contrived, through which we descended by cramp-irons or spiral stairways;—these pits again conducted us into other chambers, opening into other corridors, likewise decorated with painted sparrow-hawks, serpents coiled in circles, the symbols of the *tau* and *pedum*—prodigious works of art which no living eye can ever examine—interminable legends of granite which only the dead have time to read through all eternity.

At last we found ourselves in a hall so vast, so enormous, so immeasurable, that the eye could not reach its limits; files of monstrous columns stretched far out of sight on every side, between which twinkled livid stars of yellowish flame;—points of light which revealed further depths incalculable in the darkness beyond.

The Princess Hermonthis still held my hand, and graciously saluted the mummies of her acquaintance.

My eyes became accustomed to the dim twilight; and objects became discernible.

I beheld the kings of the subterranean races seated upon thrones—grand old men, though dry, withered, wrinkled like parchment, and blackened with naptha and bitumen—all wearing *pshents* of gold, and breastplates and gorgets glittering with precious stones; their eyes immovably fixed like the eyes of sphinxes, and their long beards whitened by the snow of centuries. Behind them stood their peoples, in the stiff and constrained posture enjoined by Egyptian art, all eternally preserving the attitude prescribed by the hieratic code. Behind these nations, the cats, ibises, and crocodiles cotemporary with them—rendered monstrous of aspect by their swathing bands—mewed, flapped their wings, or extended their jaws in a saurian giggle.

All the Pharaohs were there—Cheops, Chephrenes, Psammetichus, Sesostris, Amenotaph—all the dark rulers of the pyramids and syrinxes: —on yet higher thrones sat Chronos and Xisouthros—who was contemporary with the deluge; and Tubal Cain, who reigned before it.

The beard of King Xisouthros had grown seven times around the granite table, upon which he leaned, lost in deep reverie—and buried in dreams.

Further back, through a dusty cloud, I beheld dimly the seventy-two Preadamite Kings, with their seventy-two peoples—forever passed away.

After permitting me to gaze upon this bewildering spectacle a few moments, the Princess Hermonthis presented me to her father Pharaoh, who favored me with a most gracious nod.

"I have found my foot again!—I have found my foot!" cried the princess, clapping her little hands together with every sign of frantic joy: "it was this gentleman who restored it to me."

The races of Kemi, the races of Nahasi—all the black, bronzed, and copper-colored nations repeated in chorus:

dressing myself hurriedly; "we will go there at once; I have the permit lying there on my desk." I started to find it;—but fancy my astonishment when I beheld, instead of the mummy's foot I had purchased the evening before, the little green paste idol left in its place by the Princess Hermonthis!

THE END OF CANDIA

BY GABRIELE D'ANNUNZIO

napkins, and towels; she made the mistress take note that each piece was intact, and then passed them over to Maria, who laid them away in the drawers, while the mistress sprinkled lavender between them and entered the numbers in a book. Candia was a tall, lean, angular woman of fifty, with back somewhat bent from the habitual attitude of her calling, with arms of unusual length, and the head of a bird of prey mounted on a turtle's neck. Maria Bisaccia was a native of Ortona, a trifle stout, with a fresh complexion and the clearest of eyes; she had a soft fashion of speech, and the light, leisurely touch of one whose hands were almost always busy over cakes and sirups, pastry and preserves. Donna Cristina, also an Ortonese, and educated in a Benedictine convent, was of small stature, with a somewhat too generous expanse of bosom, a face overstrewn with freckles, a large, long nose, poor teeth, and handsome eyes cast downward in a way that made one think of a priest in woman's clothing.

The three women were performing their task with the utmost care, giving up to it the greater part of the afternoon. All at once, just as Candia was leaving with the empty baskets, Donna Cristina, in the course of counting the small silver, found that a spoon was missing.

"Maria! Maria!" she cried, in utter dismay, "count these! There's a spoon missing! Count them yourself!"

"But how could it? That's impossible, Signora!" replied Maria, "let me have a look." And she in turn began to count the small pieces, telling off the numbers aloud, while Donna Cristina looked on, shaking her head. The silver gave forth a clear, ringing sound.

"Well, it's a fact!" Maria exclaimed at last, with a gesture of despair; "what's to be done about it!"

She herself was safe from all suspicion. For fifteen years she had given proofs of her fidelity and honesty in this very household. She had come from Ortona together with Donna Cristina at the time of the wedding, almost as though she were a part of the marriage settlement; and from the first she had acquired a certain authority in the house, through the indulgence of her mistress. She was full of religious superstitions, devoted to the saint and the belfry of her birthplace, and possessed of great shrewdness. She and her mistress had formed a sort of offensive alliance against Pescara and all pertaining to it, and more particularly against the saint of the Pescarese. She never missed a chance to talk of her native town, to vaunt its beauty and its riches, the splendor of its basilica, the treasures of San Tommaso, the magnificence of its religious ceremonies, as compared with the poverty of San Cetteo, that possessed only one single little silver cross.

Donna Cristina said:

"But I didn't discharge her. Whom could I get? Silvestra?"

"Oh! oh!"

"Angelantonia? The African?"

"Each one worse than the other!"

"We must put up with it."

"But it's a spoon this time!"

"That's a little too much!"

"Don't you let it pass, Donna Cristina, don't you let it pass!"

"Let it pass, or not let it pass!" burst forth Maria Bisaccia, who, in spite of her placid and benign appearance, never let an opportunity pass for displaying her superiority over her fellow servants. "That is for us to decide, Donna Isabella, that is for us to decide!"

And the chatter continued to flow back and forth from windows to balcony. And the accusation spread from lip to lip throughout the whole countryside.

II

The following morning, Candia Marcanda already had her arms in a tubful of clothes, when the village constable, Biagio Pesce, nicknamed the Little Corporal, appeared at her door.

"His Honor, the mayor, wants you up at his office right away," he told the laundress.

"What's that?" demanded Candia, wrinkling her brows into a frown, yet without interrupting the task before her.

THE END OF CANDIA

"His Honor, the mayor, wants you up at his office, right away."

"Wants me? What does he want me for?" Candia demanded rather sharply, for she was at a loss to understand this unexpected summons, and it turned her as stubborn as a horse balking at a shadow.

"I can't tell you what for," replied the Little Corporal, "those were my orders."

"What were your orders?" From an obstinacy that was natural to her, she would not cease from asking questions. She could not convince herself that it was a reality. "The mayor wants me? What for? What have I done, I should like to know? I'm not going. I haven't done anything."

The Little Corporal, losing his temper, answered: "Oh, you won't go, won't you? We'll see about that!" and he went off, muttering, with his hand upon the hilt of the ancient sword he wore.

Meanwhile there were others along the narrow street who had overheard the conversation and came out upon their doorsteps, where they could watch Candia vigorously working her arms up and down in the tubful of clothes. And since they knew about the silver spoon, they laughed meaningly and interchanged ambiguous phrases, which Candia could not understand. But this laughter and these phrases awoke a vague foreboding in the woman's mind. And this forbod-

353

ing gathered strength when the Little Corporal reappeared, accompanied by another officer.

"Step lively," said the Little Corporal peremptorily.

Candia wiped her arms, without replying, and went with them. In the public square, people stopped to look. One of her enemies, Rosa Panura, called out from the door of her shop, with a hateful laugh: "Drop your stolen bone!"

The laundress, dazed by this persecution for which she could find no reason, was at a loss for a reply.

Before the mayor's office a group of curious idlers had gathered to watch her as she went in. Candia, in an access of anger, mounted the steps in a rush and burst into the mayor's presence, breathlessly demanding: "Well, what is it you want of me?"

Don Silla, a man of peaceful proclivities, was for the moment perturbed by the laundress's strident tones, and cast a glance at the two faithful custodians of his official dignity. Then, taking a pinch of tobacco from his horn snuff-box, he said to her: "My daughter, be seated."

But Candia remained standing. Her beak-like nose was inflated with anger, and her wrinkled cheeks quivered curiously. "Tell me, Don Silla."

"You went yesterday to take back the wash to Donna Cristina Lamonica?"

"Well, and what of it? What of it? Was

there anything missing? All of it counted, piece by piece—and not a thing missing. What's the matter with it now?"

"Wait a moment, my daughter! In the same room there was the table silver—"

Candia, comprehending, turned like an angry hawk, about to swoop upon its prey. Her thin lips twitched convulsively.

"The silver was in the room, and Donna Cristina found that a spoon was missing. Do you understand, my daughter? Could you have taken it—by mistake?"

Candia jumped like a grasshopper before the injustice of this accusation. As a matter of fact she had stolen nothing.

"Oh, it was I, was it? I? Who says so? Who saw me? I am astonished at you, Don Silla! I am astonished at you! I, a thief? I? I?"

And there was no end to her indignation. She was all the more keenly stung by the unjust charge, because she knew herself to be capable of the action they attributed to her.

"Then it was you who took it?" interrupted Don Silla, prudently sinking back into the depths of his spacious judicial chair.

"I am astonished at you!" snarled the woman once more, waving her long arms around as though they had been two sticks.

"Very well, you may go. We will see about it."

Candia went out without a salutation, blindly bumping into the doorpost. She had turned fairly green; she was beside herself. As she set foot in the street and saw the crowd which had gathered, she realized that already public opinion was against her; that no one was going to believe in her innocence. Nevertheless, she began to utter a vociferous denial. The crowd continued to laugh as it dispersed. Full of fury, she returned home, and hopelessly began to weep upon her doorstep.

Don Donato Brandimarte, who lived next door, said mockingly: "Cry louder, cry louder! There are people passing by!"

Since there were heaps of clothing still waiting for the suds, she finally calmed herself, bared her arms, and resumed her task. As she worked, she thought out her denials, elaborated a whole system of defense, sought out in her shrewd woman's brain an ingenious method of establishing her innocence; racking her brain for specious subtleties, she had recourse to every trick of rustic dialectic to construct a line of reasoning that would convince the most incredulous.

Then, when her day's work was ended, she went out, deciding to go first to see Donna Cristina.

Donna Cristina was not to be seen. It was Maria Bisaccia who listened to Candia's flood of words, shaking her head but answering nothing, and withdrawing in dignified silence.

Next, Candia made the circuit of all her clients. To each in turn she related the occurrence, to each she unfolded her defense, continually adding some new argument, amplifying her words, growing constantly more excited, more desperate, in the face of incredulity and distrust. And all in vain; she felt that from now on there was no further defense possible. A sort of blind hopelessness took possession of her—what more was there to do? What more was there to say?

III

Meanwhile Donna Cristina Lamonica gave orders to send for Cinigia, a woman of the people, who practised magic and empirical medicine with considerable success. Cinigia had several times before discovered stolen goods; and it was said that she was secretly in league with the thieves.

"Find that spoon for me," Donna Cristina told her, "and you shall have a big reward."

"Very well," Cinigia replied; "twenty-four hours are all I need."

And twenty-four hours later she brought back her answer; the spoon was to be found in a hole in the courtyard, near the well.

Donna Cristina and Maria descended to the courtyard, made search, and, to their great amazement, found the spoon.

Swiftly the news spread throughout Pescara.

Then triumphantly Candia Marcanda went the rounds of all the streets. She seemed to have grown taller; she held her head erect; she smiled, looking every one straight in the eye, as if to say, "I told you so! I told you so!"

The people in the shops, seeing her pass by, would murmur something and then break forth into a significantly sneering laugh. Filippo La Selvi, who sat drinking a glass of liqueur brandy in the Café d'Ange, called Candia in.

"Another glass for Candia, the same as mine!"

The woman, who was fond of strong spirits, pursed up her lips covetously.

"You certainly deserve it, there's no denying that!" added Filippo La Selvi.

An idle crowd had gathered in front of the café. They all had the spirit of mischief in their faces. While the woman drank, Filippo La Selvi turned and addressed his audience:

"Say, she knew how to work it, didn't she? Isn't she the foxy one?" and he slapped the laundress familiarly upon her bony shoulder.

The crowd laughed. A little dwarf, called Magnafave, or "Big Beans," weak-minded and stuttering, joined the forefinger of his right hand to that of his left, and striking a grotesque attitude and dwelling upon each syllable, said:

"Ca—ca—ca—Candia—Ci—ci—Cinigia!" and he continued to make gestures and to stammer forth vulgar witticisms, all implying that Candia and Cinigia were in league together. His spectators indulged in contortions of merriment.

For a moment Candia sat there bewildered,

with the glass still in her hand. Then in a flash she understood—they did not believe in her innocence. They accused her of having brought back the silver spoon secretly, by agreement with the sorceress, to save herself further trouble.

An access of blind anger came upon her. Speechless with passion, she flung herself upon the weakest of them, upon the little hunchback, in a hurricane of blows and scratches. And the crowd, at the sight of this struggle, formed a circle and jeered at them in cruel glee, as at a fight between two animals, and egged on the two combatants with voice and gesture.

Big Beans, badly scared by her unexpected violence, tried to escape, hopping about like a little ape; and held fast by the laundress's terrible arms, whirled round and round with increasing velocity, like a stone in a sling, until at last he fell violently upon his face.

Some of the men hastened to pick him up. Candia withdrew in the midst of hisses, shut herself within her house, and flung herself across her bed, sobbing and gnawing her fingers, in the keenness of her suffering. The new accusation cut her deeper than the first, and all the more that she knew herself capable of such a subterfuge. How was she to clear herself now? How was she to establish the truth? She grew hopeless as she realized that she could not allege in defense any material difficulties that might have interfered with carrying out the deception. Access to the courtyard was perfectly simple; a door, that was never fastened, opened from the ground floor of the main stairway; people came and went freely through that door, to remove the garbage, or for other causes. So it was impossible for her to close the lips of her accusers by saying, "How could I have got in?" The means of successfully carrying out such a plan were many and easy.

Candia proceeded to conjure up new arguments to convince them; she sharpened up her wits; she invented three, four, five different cases to prove that the spoon never could have been found in that hole in the courtyard; she split hairs with marvelous ingenuity. Next she took to making the rounds of the shops and the houses, seeking in every possible way to overcome the people's incredulity. They listened to her, greatly entertained by her captious reasoning; and they would end by saying, "Oh, it's all right!"

But there was a certain tone in their voice that left Candia annihilated. So, then, all her trouble was for nothing! No one would believe her! Yet with marvelous persistence she would return to the attack, spending whole nights in thinking out new arguments. And little by little, under this continued strain, her mind gave way; she could no longer follow any sustained thought but that of the silver spoon.

Neglecting her work, she had sunk to a state of

actual want. When she went down to the river
bank, under the iron bridge, where the other
wash-women congregated, she would sometimes
let slip from between her fingers the garments
that the current swept away forever. And she
would talk continually, unweariedly, of the one
single subject. In order not to hear her, the
young laundresses would begin to sing, and
would mock her with the improvised rimes of
their songs. And she meanwhile would shout and
gesticulate like a crazy woman.

No one could give her work any longer. Out
of pity, some of her former employers would
send her food. Little by little she fell into the
habit of begging, and wandered through the
streets, bowed over, unkempt, and all in rags.
The street urchins would tag behind her, shouting: "Tell us the story of the spoon," 'cause we
never heard it, Auntie Candia!"

She would stop strangers sometimes as they
passed by, to tell them the story and to argue out
her defense. Young fellows would sometimes
send for her, and pay her a copper to tell it all
over, two, three, or four times; they would raise
up difficulties against her arguments; they would
hear her all the way through, and then at last
stab her with a final word. She would shake her
head, and go on her way; she found companion-
ship among other beggars and would reason with
them endlessly, indefatigably, invincibly. Her
chosen friend was a deaf woman, whose skin was

a mass of angry blotches, and who limped on one 'eg.

In the winter of 1874 she was at last stricken with serious illness. The woman with the blotches cared for her. Donna Cristina Lamonica sent her a cordial and a scuttle of coals.

The sick woman, lying on her pallet, still raved of the silver spoon. She would raise herself on her elbow and struggle to wave her arm, to give emphasis to her fevered arguments.

And at the last, when her staring eyes already seemed overspread with a veil of troubled waters that rose from within, Candia gasped forth:

"It wasn't I, madam—because you see—the spoon—"

THE PRICE OF A LIFE

BY AUGUSTIN EUGÈNE SCRIBE

THE PRICE OF A LIFE

BY AUGUSTIN EUGENE SCRIBE

JOSEPH, opening the door of the salon, came to tell us that the post-chaise was ready. My mother and my sister threw themselves into my arms. "There is yet time," said they. "It is not too late. Give up this journey and remain with us." I replied: "My mother, I am a gentleman. I am twenty years old, my country needs me, I must win fame and renown; be it in the army, be it at court, I must be heard of, men must speak of me."

"And when you are far away, tell me, Bernard, what will become of me, your old mother?"

"You will be happy and proud to hear of your son's successes—"

"And if you are killed in some battle?"

"What matters it? What is life? Only a dream. One dreams only of glory at twenty, and when one is a gentleman; but do not fear, you will see me return to you in a few years, a colonel, a maréchal-de-camp, or, better still, with a fine position at Versailles."

"Indeed! When will that be?"

"It will come, and I shall be respected and